SOON
THE
DAWN

LINDA BROOKS DAVIS

INSPIRATION

He that dwelleth in the secret place of the Most High
Shall abide under the shadow of the Almighty.
Psalm 91:1 ASV

DEDICATION

To

Jennifer and McKenna

Many daughters have done well, But you excel them all.
Proverbs 31:29 NKJV
I love you.

IN MEMORY

Papa

William Tribble Banks

1880-1922
I've waited a lifetime to tell your story. I love you.

CHAPTER ONE

Thy lovingkindness, O Jehovah, is in the heavens;
Thy faithfulness reacheth unto the skies.
Psalm 36:5

31 January 1906
Needham, Indian Territory

Who's that knocking?" I flicked aside a curtain panel. A Model T was parked in the driveway, and a group of strangers huddled on the front porch. "A woman I've never seen. And a passel of kids. Who are they, for heaven's sake?"

"I'll see, Ella. Go ahead with breakfast." Andrew slipped on his coat and swung open the door.

I wiped my hands on my apron and sidled next to my husband. Breakfast could wait.

A matron in a humble black hat stood straight as a starched collar and held a months-old babe sporting a pink hair bow. The woman's silvery wisps were slicked into a bun. Four little girls—two toddlers and a pair not yet school-age—held onto her skirt on either side.

Who were these people?

Andrew welcomed them with his characteristic good humor. "Hello. Looks like your hands're full." He reached for the dark- and abundant-haired baby. "May I help you?"

She relinquished the child with a deep sigh. "I'm Gertrude Goss. Folks call me Widow Goss. But you can call me Gertrude.

I'm with Indian Territory's Office of Charities. Three different families have considered adopting these children. Separately, I might add. But nothing worked. These girls simply cannot thrive separately."

Andrew motioned our unexpected guests inside. "Makes sense to me. But what can we do?"

"You can adopt them." She spouted the words as if they were trivial.

"Adopt them?" we chorused in unison.

I pressed a hand over my chest. "We've only been married a month, ma'am. Just returned from our honeymoon."

The children's expressions were strained.

"What am I thinking?" Andrew nodded toward our spacious living space. "Please. Have a seat."

We stood aside, and the woman all but collapsed onto the divan. The girls scrambled alongside her with skirts and pinafores, arms and legs akimbo.

I scurried to the stove and poured a cup of coffee. "Have a cup, Gertrude." Setting it on a side table, I bent toward the four youngsters, one with her thumb in her mouth. "Want something to eat?"

They nodded, and I seated them at the kitchen table with buttered toast and milk. I gawked at the little darlings. All were bright haired—one with curls, another with waves, and two with long, corn-silk strands. And light-eyed in variegated tones from sky- to denim- to aquamarine blue. I suspected their ages ranged from two to five years.

What perfectly adorable children.

Our living and dining rooms and kitchen comprised one large space we called our family room. We could eat our meals at the kitchen table, huddle before the fire on the divan, or gather with family and friends around our oak dining table, all in the same room.

Andrew eased into his Morris armchair with the bundle of pink tucked into the crook of his arm. "We're in no position to take on five children. We're newlyweds." Frown lines deepened on his forehead. "Who sent you to us?"

"The chairman of the board. Worthington School for Girls. Said you were familiar with this family and that . . ." She focused on Andrew's empty left sleeve. "You may be one-armed, but you're certainly not disabled. He assured me you're perfectly capable of rearing these girls."

Bouncing the now-fussy infant, my husband angled his head to the side. "I beg your pardon. I have no idea who these children are."

The woman flicked both hands. "They're the Hanson girls. You know . . ."

My husband stared, as if struggling to connect the dots.

"Their mother died of consumption last year, and soon after, their hard-of-hearing father was caught in the path of an oncoming train in a raging storm." She *tsk-tsked*.

Lucidity returned to Andrew's countenance. "Oh. Yes. I *am* familiar with this family."

She expelled a sigh. "Thank God."

Andrew cast me a pleading expression to which I could only shrug. "You say the chairman of the board sent you, Gertrude?"

"Indeed." She returned her cup to its saucer, and the china clattered. "He said he knew you well." She glanced in my direction. "Gave his unabashed approval of both of you."

She peered at Andrew's dangling sleeve. "The appropriate authorities approved the placement despite your infirmity and pending my visit, of course." She angled her eyes left and right across the room's broad expanse. "Your home is perfectly cozy."

The baby fussed and squirmed in Andrew's unfamiliar embrace. He gave her a sturdier bounce. "Yes, but—"

"Looks like you have plenty of space." She pointed overhead and rose. "May I see?"

Obviously at a loss for words, Andrew joined her at the foot of the staircase.

"You lead the way, young man."

He nodded and took to the stairs with the infant in arm. The baby *gooed* over his shoulder, and Gertrude's prim footsteps followed.

Meanwhile, the girls had finished their snack and begged me to hold them.

"Let's see what's upstairs." I cleaned their hands and led the miniature quartet up the staircase, one cautious step and another. While I observed in the broad upper hallway, the little ones held onto the folds of my skirt.

Gertrude scurried about with her mouth ajar. "Oh my. There's a room for each of them. Look at that, beds for all."

"Our friends and family have been more than generous." I closed a door and trailed her.

"I'll say." She peeked out a side window. "Lookey there. A horse barn. Outbuildings." She turned her eagle eyes on me. "That's a good well, isn't it?"

"Always has been. Since the Fitzgeralds dug it decades ago."

She tapped a fingertip on the window glass. "Over there's a garden. Do you can vegetables?"

"Indeed. Canning's a part of rural life."

She pointed toward the east with a puzzled expression. "That's a magnificent home over the way. Just glimpsed it coming in. The home of a famous opera star, is it not?"

I held out a hand, signifying our exit from the room. "It is. She's been in Italy several years, but she's home now."

The woman pressed both hands over her bosom. "You mean she'll be performing in Indian Territory?"

"Not sure about that. What had lured me into a chat about my best friend? "Let's go downstairs. We've a great deal to discuss."

She *humphed*. "Indeed." Wasting not a moment, she returned to the living room and settled onto the divan.

Andrew took his easy chair. It provided space for his tall frame as well as the infant now snoozing on his chest.

"Surely your coffee's grown cold, Gertrude," I said. "May I pour you a fresh cup?"

"No thank you, dear." She handed me the empty cup and extended her hands toward Andrew. "Here. Give me Ebony."

He relinquished the babe, and the girls dashed for him. Shooting them a grin and a wink, he allowed them to crawl onto his lap.

"Move, Blossom," the eldest said, pushing her sister aside.

"It's too crowded, Amy."

"My name's Am-a-ryl-lis, Blossom." She twisted from the knot of sisters and slid onto the arm of the chair as gracefully as a swan.

Meanwhile, Gertrude struggled with the now squirming infant.

"Here. Let me take her." I tugged the child into my arms and settled into a matching armchair. What a warm and cuddly bundle.

Arms askew, the lemony-haired sisters soon snoozed on Andrew's chest. "They must be tired. How far did you drive today, Gertrude?" he whispered.

"Drove from Worthington. Little contraption purred steady all the way. Took over two hours, what with stopping to tend the children now and again."

I gave the baby's bottom a pat. "You're a brave soul."

"*Pshaw*. All in a good day's work. I've a long list of others to look after." She grinned. "Five less, now that these cherubs have found a home."

Had this woman any idea what she was asking of us? Married only a month. Andrew still adjusting to his *infirmity*, as she called it. And both of us feeling our way in married life. Taking on five girls was impossible.

What in the world were she and the board chairman thinking? "We can't possibly make a home for these girls. Even one child would—"

Andrew cleared his throat and speared me with his gaze. "It appears these girls feel at home already."

At *home*? Don't tell me my husband had been caught in…

He nodded to the dumpling sleeping on my chest and flashed his *We-can-do-it-dear* smile.

Truly, could we give these girls the life they deserved?

What about my own Broadview School for Girls, the calling on my life? Could I do it all?

When these girls' adulthood arrives, could I let them go? Time and again, I had pushed God aside and steered my life in my own way. Could I trust Him with my family?

I gazed down at the pink-blanketed bundle and experienced a rush of warmth from my middle to my crown. Could this be the mysterious emotion folks talked about, the affection of a mother?

"This is Ebony, you say, Gertrude?" I traced the child's profile with a fingertip and found myself smiling.

CHAPTER TWO

*For Jehovah is good; his lovingkindness endureth forever,
And his faithfulness unto all generations.*
Psalm 100:5

New Year's Eve 1921
Needham, Oklahoma

Our sixteenth wedding anniversary.

The years had slipped by without our notice. In a single winter's day in 1906, we had become a family of seven. And in the fall of the same year, we had welcomed our own raven-haired daughter, Julia Jane. Happier than eight speckled pups at a bowl of warm milk, we had gobbled up the joy and contentment in loving one another.

Today's dry, forty-degree weather meant Andrew and I could wrap in quilts and nestle in the porch swing, our sacred spot for musing on ordinary things—like the silvery haze around a winter moon, a child's long-ago loss of a first tooth, or a new colt wobbling on toothpick legs.

My husband and I stepped onto our front porch with quilts around our shoulders and knitting covering our heads, hands, and feet. He carried a beaver throw to luxuriate in thoughts of endless days of contentment.

"Look." I pointed to the stars peeking through the clear black canopy above. "Aren't they beautiful?"

Contentment rumbled in his chest. "Scripture says the

morning stars sing over God's creation. Thirty-eighth chapter of Job, if I remember right. Singing stars are extraordinary to us, but they appear to be commonplace in heaven."

"A not-so-ordinary consideration—our Amy—strains at her tethers." I laid my head over his heart. "Her dear face first brightened this porch only yesterday, it seems. And now, she'll be twenty-one in May." All born in May, the five sisters had been named for the beauty in their first mother's garden: Amaryllis, Blossom, Camellia, Dahlia, and Ebony.

"With Amy's graduation and all their birthdays the same month, except Julia Jane's of course, May will be memorable for all five." The eldest four attended College of Industrial Arts in Denton, Texas, and I schooled our other two in my own Broadview School for Girls.

"Amy'll be like a filly on the first day of spring." A chuckle rippled in Andrew's chest, and then he sobered. "Mother wants her to return to Denver with them, you know."

My middle tightened at the mention of Josephine Evans. "I didn't know." My mother-in-law often failed to inform me of her plans for my daughter.

"Mother asked when she called last. I forgot to tell you, Ella. I'm sorry."

"When Amy's included in your m— in Denver's society circles, she gets uppity. Have you noticed?" Our firstborn, pretty in a quiet way, basked in the society dames' attention.

He *humphed*. "I don't want our girls to take on Mother's socialite ways. But I think making Amy the center of attention for a couple of weeks will be good for her."

I sighed. "Favoritism in any form always ends in trouble. Will you speak with your mother about waiting until Amy graduates? And perhaps doing something special with the others soon?"

"I'll call her at the hotel tomorrow, dear." Andrew's affluent parents, Josephine and Owen, routinely booked a suite at Needham Hotel.

A barn owl hooted a lullaby, and I looked up at my husband, eager to think on more pleasant subjects. "That feathered mama and papa are putting their babies to bed. Do you think owls say bedtime prayers?"

He laughed. "Living near this family, surely they do."

A coyote howled in the distance, and another answered. I drew myself closer to my beloved "You have a strong, steady heartbeat."

"It would stop beating altogether without you. My heart's dry kindling, and you're the match that sets it ablaze."

"I feel the same, dear. More than ever before."

"I want Jesus' love to set our girls' hearts ablaze for Him, their eternal husband."

I nodded. "Their First Love."

"When our girls primp at their mirrors, I pray they'll see they're God's handiwork. Nothing about them is without cause, so He has a plan for each of them. That's His hand of purpose."

Was my husband intending his observations for the girls? Or me? "And the ebony on our mantelpiece?"

"His hand of providence. Our girls must trust Him to guide them, or they'll get lost, sure as the world. Their influence for good depends on it."

Years ago, I'd fought off a rabid dog with the pocked ebony limb, and Andrew had insisted we keep it as an Ebenezer of sorts, a reminder of God's providential care. He had carved the first verse of Psalm 91 into the wood and set it on the mantel above the fireplace: *He that dwelleth in the secret place of the Most High shall abide under the shadow of the Almighty.*

"The Almighty's got us in the hollow of His hand, and His shadow's covering us, love."

Andrew was speaking to me. Did I trust that psalm? Even with my family?

As we absorbed the sounds of this last night of 1921, darkness settled around us like a boiled-wool cape. Again, a coyote howled, and his mate called back.

An ever-rising chill came on tiptoes and gripped us. Soon we yearned for the warmth of our cozy cottage, so we joined our daughters inside. All six had sprawled on divans, chaise lounges, and cowhide rugs before the fire.

"Didn't make it to twelve o'clock." Andrew reached out to awaken Amaryllis.

"Let them sleep. Who knows, with Amy straining at the bit to be set free and Denver calling, this could be their last New Year's Eve together.

"Alright. We'll wake them in time to welcome the new year."

"Meanwhile, Andrew dear, cider's simmering."

He followed on my heels. "Coffee too?"

I turned and eyed him under a raised eyebrow. "Of course."

"Will you set out those buttery balls?" His crystal-clear blue eyes sparkled.

"The Mexican wedding cookies? They're always on our holiday menu." As I poured my husband a mug of hot black coffee, aromatic swirls drifted toward the ceiling. I recalled with pleasure the migrant Espinosa family who had lived nearby before world war knocked eight years ago.

Slurping at his mug's rim, he slipped a ball of rich sweetness into his mouth and closed his eyes. "Ahh."

I joined him at the table and nodded toward our brood. "Our girls seem to pair off, don't they?"

"You're right. Amy and Blossom. Camy and Dolly. Ebony and JJ."

"They complement one another. Amy's reticence tones down Blossom's enthusiasm."

"Dolly's toughness balances out Camy's tears."

"And Ebony and JJ are our two proverbial peas in a pod."

A half hour before midnight, the girls stirred.

"Is it time yet?"

"You stole my covers."

"In self-defense."

"Would you please be quiet?"

"How can you sleep at a time like this?"

"1922 is on our doorstep, sisters!"

At the stroke of twelve, they cheered and threw confetti but soon retreated to their rooms, droopy-eyed.

Andrew and I slipped into the warmth of the bed we had shared for sixteen years. Anticipating the blessings 1922 had in store for our family, we nestled in one another's arms and welcomed dreamless slumber.

CHAPTER THREE

For thou wilt bless the righteous;
O Jehovah, thou wilt compass him with favor, as with a shield.
Psalm 5:12

New Year's Day 1922

I awoke with an unfamiliar sense of dread.
Rising before the sun, I grabbed a flashlight from the mud room and scurried to Mama and Papa's place on the other side of a thick copse. A light rain overnight, together with the freezing temperature, had created a fine layer of ice. Thankfully, the pebbled pathway held me in good stead.

The kitchen light burned brightly through windowpanes Mama kept sparkling, even with the crippling arthritis that gnarled her hands and bent her back. I had something on my mind that only a talk with Mama could remedy.

Papa excused himself to putter in the barn, and I pulled a straight-backed chair alongside my mother.

She set aside her sewing basket. "Something's troubling you, daughter mine. What is it?"

"Not completely sure. Could be my mother-in-law."

"Don't tell me her socialite ways are still eating at you, child."

"Not regarding myself . . ."

"Who then?"

"Josephine plans to take her eldest granddaughter to

Denver for a couple weeks, and Amy's stirring like a bubbling pot. She's packed and ready to go. Rather than thinking about her last semester in college, she's anticipating what a fine time she'll have in that far-off city. I possess not an iota of peace about it."

"What about her schooling?"

"They don't reconvene for the second term until later this month. Her grandparents will send her back in plenty of time."

"She'll travel all the way from Denver alone?"

I sighed. "Maybe that's what's troubling me. But she's nigh onto twenty-one now. Time to loosen my apron strings a bit."

Mama nodded, sage-like, and took my hand.

I leaned closer. "Just last night I fell asleep thinking about all the blessings God has in store for us this coming year." I ran my fingers through the strand of curls that had fallen over my shoulder. "And here I am, nursing an unfamiliar foreboding."

She sat back, pulled out her weaving loom, and set her fingers to tapestry-making. "You know troubles can come on us at any time."

"Of course. I've learned a thing or two in thirty-eight years. Our losses of the past aside, I'm counting on the Lord to bless us from now on."

"Don't expect Him to do your bidding, daughter. He tests those that love him." She gave a one-shoulder shrug. "Could be He'll mold you by fire."

"That's a dreadful thought, Mama. Andrew's loss of an arm, little Andrew's dying before he had a chance to thrive, and our precious twin boys in the ground before they took their first breaths, isn't that enough loss for one lifetime?"

"Keep in mind that all folks suffer hard times like yours. If more come to you, I pray you'll remember the stream out yonder." She thumbed toward the north.

I smiled. "How could I forget Papa's wisdom? Heard it often enough. 'Weren't for the rocks, the creek wouldn't make a sound. They give it its voice.'"

"Same's true of God's people. Troubles give us our best voice. Mighty easy to get comfortable in good times and forget who gave them to us."

I lowered my head to Mama's shoulder, and she reached up and patted my cheek. "Run along now. I reckon you got a few things to do today."

Returning along the pathway through the copse, I chased pesky thoughts down rabbit trails strewn with the unknown. I must set aside this gloom.

When I stepped onto the back porch, dawn was just spreading hopefulness over the horizon. A good sign.

Andrew had yet to rise. I lit the gas stove and set a pot of coffee to boil. Prepared a ham for baking, spearing its surface with pineapple slices, bright red cherries, and dried cloves. And slid it into the oven. Our New Year's meal would be a simple one that consisted of ham, black-eyed peas, and greens. I'd prepare a pan of cornbread later.

We would attend a brief ten o'clock church service without Andrew's parents. His mother had insisted she hadn't time for a backward church out nowhere. Andrew would pick them up after church for dinner at our home.

Stepping into our bedroom, I found Andrew out of bed and buttoning his shirt. "Where you been, Ella?"

"Visiting with Mama."

"She doing alright?"

"Pretty good. I fear she's constantly in pain, though."

He nodded. "I'll pray for her." He tucked his shirttail into his trousers and pulled up his suspenders. "Looks like something's on your mind. Come with me to the study. We can talk."

"It'll be cold as a crypt. Better bundle up."

"I'll go on out and start the fire."

I nodded and pulled on thick stockings and a woolen split skirt. With my mane of thick curls wrapped into a haphazard bun, I tugged on a stocking cap, gloves, and boots.

As I entered the study, Andrew was returning the fire iron to its rack. He rubbed his soiled hand on a pant leg and pulled a divan with crocheted throws near the fire. Cocooned in my and Mama's handwork, we huddled together at one end of the couch.

Flinging off my cap and unpinning my bun, he secured my head beneath his chin and ran his fingers through my mop. "Something on your mind, dear?"

I must take care not to allow the subjects of Josephine and Denver to create a wedge between us. She was his mother, after all. "It's Amy."

"You're worrying about Mother's influence."

"I wouldn't put it like that exactly." How I would put it would do our relationship no good.

He drew me nearer. "How would you put it then?"

I caught a deep breath and let it out with a silent prayer. *Help me find words that fit.* "You and I both know how Amy changes after she's been with your mother's social crowd. And now that she's on the verge of independence, I fear how she might be tempted."

"I know you, dear. You're worried Mother has her sights set on marrying our eldest to the son of one of her compatriots. Amy will be pondering some handsome fellow in Denver and entertaining wedding dreams rather than finishing college"

I glowered before the truth I had hidden. "All right, dear. I am worried I'll lose Amy to Josephine. But even if she returns, she'll come back distracted. I just know it. I'd like her to keep her eyes on her goal, graduation. And enjoy her friends before they go their separate ways."

He *humphed*. "Would you have Amy unpack?"

"Oh, Andrew. When you put it like that . . ."

"Let's think through this, dear. We'll already pointed Amy to Song of Solomon."

"That doesn't help a bit. The book's brimming over with lovers' talk."

"Granted. But it's a metaphor for God's love for us, His bride; so, consider this. Amy takes Jesus into her heart as if He were her husband. We accept Him as her guardian, her protector, her eternal love. And then we relax."

"Easy for you to say."

"Oh?"

"Men don't understand. Mother-love is in a category of its own."

"I'm only concerned with *this* mother." He tapped a finger on my chest. "And our daughter. Can you do it, Ella? Can you trust Jesus with Amy?"

We sat several moments in silence within our homemade cocoon.

He continued to probe. "Do you think God's taken care of us this past year?"

"Of course. When I look back on 1921, I see a passel of blessings."

"Think you can trust Him with 1922, even with Amy in Denver?"

I don't know what it is about a sigh, but at the end of a long, deep one, I feel as if I've dumped a year's worth of garbage off a ridge. So, I sighed and felt better prepared for where the discussion was headed.

Loosening myself from his embrace, I sat up. "God was around last year. And He's not taking a vacation in 1922, not even in Denver."

He kissed me on the cheek. "That's great news, dear. Now

we can see Amy off with smiles on our faces and joy in our hearts."

My, how Andrew could chew every morsel off a bone and leave me nothing to gnaw on.

CHAPTER FOUR

Come, ye children, hearken unto me:
I will teach you the fear of Jehovah.
Psalm 34:11

B ath time had always been a challenge in our female-dom-
inated home. We had extended water from Broadview's
system to the cottage, but occasionally we used our old
well. This Sunday morning, everyone needed baths at the same
time, so Amaryllis brought in well water for herself.

She poured a glassful and gulped down the crystal-clear
liquid. "Funny tasting," she said as if puzzled.

"You're too excited to know what you're tasting." I heated
the water to a comfortable temperature and poured it into a tin
tub in the mud room.

When Amaryllis and the other girls had washed up and
dressed for church, she led her sisters downstairs. Skipping like
a ten-year-old headed to a picnic, she scooted out the door
ahead of the rest of us.

Thankfully, Andrew had left the auto idling and floor
heaters humming. When Adelaide had married in 1919, she had
left Broadview's Pierce Arrow limousine with us. A flashy con-
veyance like President Wilson's, it was designed to seat seven,
but we Evanses found space for eight.

Andrew scraped the last of the icy slush off the windscreen.

SOON THE DAWN

The thermometer had read twenty-eight degrees at sunup, but by midmorning, the ice was mush.

"Brr." He slid into the driver's seat, rubbed his palm along his pant leg, and blew into his fist. "With all that's been going on this week, I found little time for sermon preparation. I've been using my study for . . ." He snapped his eyes toward me. "For decidedly more pleasant endeavors."

Suppressing a grin, I stared out the window. "Surely you have a former sermon you could dust off."

"Found one."

Hmm. My husband had a plan for this New Year's Day.

He didn't disappoint.

Setting his open Bible on the lectern, he smiled and let his gaze drift across the room. "Our Amy's graduating from college in May." Other parents nodded, but deep pink circles blazed on our daughter's cheeks. "It's a joyous time, but an uncertain one, too. I'd go so far as to say it's a troubling time for us parents."

I looked around the congregation. Knowing expressions seemed to wallpaper the room.

"Our Lord spoke on the subject of worry in the Sermon on the Mount. Check the thirty-second verse of Matthew Six where He explains that our heavenly father knows what we need. And the thirty-fourth verse. 'Be not therefore anxious for the morrow: for the morrow will be anxious for itself.'"

Closing his Bible, he stepped from the podium and positioned himself in his favorite spot—in the aisle, near the flock, with his eyes and ears trained on the sheep.

"Ella and I have encouraged our girls to read Song of Solomon this year. Oh, it's full of lovers' talk, as my wife calls it, but we know it's intended to show God's tender and passionate love for us, his bride."

I looked around, wondering if any stodgy matrons were

frowning and shaking their heads. Thankfully, all eyes were trained on the preacher, and heads bobbed here and there.

"We can trust Him to be faithful, tender, and true, as well as passionate." He raised his hand toward the ceiling, created a fist, and mimicked a hammer's five succinct blows. "He can do no other."

As his final words echoed off the bare plank walls, he held out his hand to the song leader, my twin brother, Cade. "Let's sing to the heavens and then go home and enjoy this first day of 1922."

The girls' queries about lovers' talk peppered the drive home. Their papa's bringing out such a subject in the public had loosened their tongues.

"We'll get to those explanations as we come to them, girls. Let's proceed with today's festivities and think of nothing but sending off your grandparents and Amy with joy."

He was directing the message my way too. But he needn't have worried. Oh, I still questioned why my heavenly husband would allow his wife to endure the sorrow of losing three children. Or other women to see the good men they married maimed, slaughtered, and buried way off in France. But I'd made up my mind. Jesus would take care of my six girls whether they married or not. And when sorrows came, He'll be their divine husband, carrying them through.

I didn't dare ask Andrew the final question nagging me: *How about sparing women the grief in the first place?* I'd save it for a more opportune time.

Back home, I slipped on an apron and pondered the pantry's dwindling jars of peas and greens. Although the garden had supplied what we needed thus far, I feared we'd run short before the next harvest.

The girls changed into house dresses, excepting Amaryllis, who chose to don her new traveling suit. "Grand Mama will be dressed for travel, and so will I." She tied a bibbed apron at her neck and waist and finished setting the table.

Just as I was taking cornbread from the oven, Andrew arrived with his parents. "Just in time, ya'll."

Josephine ignored me and looked to her eldest grand-daughter. "Are you packed and ready to go?"

"I've been packed for days."

Andrew gazed at Amaryllis with a tender expression and *humphed.*

"It's high time she got a taste of what life can be . . ." Josephine flicked her eyes around the family room and kitchen. "Outside *rural* environs."

Amaryllis took her grandmother's wrap. "I know all about city life, Grand Mama. Don't forget I'm in school in Denton and have been to Fort Worth many times."

Josephine raised her chin and sniffed. "Neither compares with Denver, I assure you."

We gathered around our large oak table that sported gouges and scrapes from years of family meals, crafts and art-work, and reams of homework. The ham anchored the New Year's array on a rose-encrusted platter, my anniversary gift a few years back. Matching bowls of steaming vegetables. And cornbread, piping hot.

Chickasaw plum pies and whipped cream awaited us for dessert. Best of all, the sight of my girls: four lemon drops and two chocolate bonbons.

Andrew inhaled and released a sigh. "Smells good enough to eat." He blessed the food and our loved ones' upcoming journey.

We ate our fill, and the girls made short work of cleaning the kitchen while Andrew visited with his parents a final time. I simply observed.

His father's real estate business continued to flourish. His brother and sister had established themselves in Denver's social circles. And his mother wondered how she'd ever fulfill all the responsibilities she'd taken on, committees she chaired, and soirees she hosted.

Her fluttering reminded me of the blue jays that nested in the oak tree out back, not the piercing *jayer-jayer* of a papa jay, but their chattering among themselves. But a layer of superiority like the squeaky *creak* of a rusty hand pump overlaid Josephine's jabber.

Forgive my uncharitable thoughts, Lord.

The girls excused themselves, and I grabbed an opportunity to speak with their grandmother. "About Amy—"

"I'll not take my eyes off her."

What fun. "I appreciate that. Have you planned sightseeing? Maybe a gathering with girls her age?"

"Amaryllis is a grown woman. It's time she entered adult circles. Developed social graces. And met eligible bachelors who can provide a secure future."

My eyes stretched wide. "Men, you mean?"

"Of course. We must consider her future."

We?

Andrew peered at me beneath eyebrows that had arched in a dramatic fashion.

I bridled my tongue. "Amy has a mind of her own, you know. She'll have earned a teaching certificate by May. And who knows where—"

"No place like Denver. We're growing like dandelions. School-aged children everywhere I look."

How could I argue?

However, I held back the words I itched to speak.

Amaryllis Evans would teach whomever and wherever— she chose.

CHAPTER FIVE

Our sons shall be as plants grown up in their youth,
And our daughters as corner-stones hewn after the fashion of a palace.
Psalm 144:12

The trip to Fair Valley was spirited, to say the least. Andrew's father Owen sat up front with him. Josephine claimed the middle seat for herself and insisted only Amaryllis sit beside her. They must protect their attire, after all. The rest of us squeezed into the back seat—I and all five girls bunched on one another's laps. I strained to hear the conversations in the other two seats, but my daughters' prattle drowned out everything else.

Andrew had hired a depot hack to transport the baggage ahead of us. When we parked the car, the condition of my mother-in-law's soft, leather luggage appeared to be her first thought. "Take me to my bags. I'll not tolerate mishandling."

She turned to her eager protégé. "Come with me, dear girl. Watch and learn."

Glancing at me, Amaryllis shrugged, and I waved her onward.

Owen escorted his wife and granddaughter to the baggage car, and the rest of us waited on platform benches.

"Watch your step, young man." Josephine's sharp instructions pierced through the waiting travelers' low murmurs. "That's fine Italian leather."

A triple whistle brought us to our feet. The train was nearing.

The rest of our band of travelers joined us, and I reached out to Amaryllis. "Let's talk over here." I motioned her to follow me to an unoccupied area that would provide privacy. "I can't let you leave without a few moments alone."

"For heaven's sakes, Mama. I'll only be gone two weeks."

I speared her with an unflinching gaze. "Two weeks in Denver could—"

"What? Ruin me?"

"Of course not."

She gave a one-shoulder shrug. "What's the matter then?"

I slipped my arm through hers. "You'll understand when you're a mother yourself. Suffice to say, my maternal intuition is nagging."

With a tender expression, she wrapped an arm around my shoulder. "You mustn't worry, Mother. I'm a grown woman. I can take care of myself."

I pointed my teacher finger at her nose. "Until you turn twenty-one and hold a diploma in your hand, your mother will watch out for you."

She chuckled. "You'll watch out for me only five more months? Can't imagine."

The train chugged near and squealed to a stop with an enormous belch of steam.

I grabbed my daughter by the shoulders and drew her nearer. "Promise me, Amy. You won't let all that social folderol change a single speck of who you are. And please be careful. Don't leave your grandmother's sight."

She belly laughed. "You think there's a chance of that?"

I returned a half smile. We eased through the cloud of vapor and stretched our necks to locate our loved ones. The girls caught sight of us and let out a stream of heckles.

"Need spectacles?"

"This locomotive is about to leave you behind, sis."

"Hurry up, poke-along."

"Grand Mama's waiting for you, Amy."

"I'll go for you if you've changed your mind."

Amaryllis waved off their banter and dispensed with final hugs.

Owen helped his wife onto the rear platform of their appointed passenger car. Cherry-red and polished to a dazzling gleam, it boasted a red-and-white striped awning. "Take my hand, dear." He reached for his granddaughter and whisked her from my side, leaving me bereft.

Andrew's arm encircled my waist. "She'll be fine, dear. Reflect her joy. For now, anyway."

I nodded and fortified myself with a deep breath. Raising a white hankie, I forced my biggest smile. "Have a safe trip, everyone."

Our beloved travelers found their compartment, and Amaryllis let down a window. She popped her head outside, and we rushed to her.

I grabbed her hand. "Goodbye, my darling. Call at least once."

"And have fun," Andrew said.

"Comport yourself like a lady." Josephine pulled Amy inside and slid up the window, leaving inches for our farewells.

The other five girls quieted and appeared to be holding back an unshed tear or two. "We'll miss you," they called in unison.

My daughter's nod through the glass struck me as somewhat subdued. Had we made a mistake, allowing this sensitive girl to travel so far from family?

She's in Your hands, Lord.

The engine released a strong belch, and the wheels

squealed into motion. It inched forward and picked up steam. Signaling a final farewell with a double whistle, it rounded a curve and faded out of sight.

Silence descended, and I lowered my hankie to my side. I'd stand here, awaiting her return, for two whole weeks if I could.

On the decidedly subdued ride home, my chickadees uttered not a single peep. Andrew attempted conversation, but I wanted nothing more than to stare out the window. Store fronts whizzed by. Farmland. Windmills. Fence lines. All faded into my daughter's robin's-egg-blue eyes.

Back home, the girls took to their separate rooms, and Andrew and I wrapped up on the porch.

He ran his forefinger along my hairline. "Proud of you, dear."

I stared at the leafless bittersweet vine that climbed the posts. "I didn't react this way when Amy went away to college."

"You could get to her by train in a couple of hours."

I sighed. "Which I've done how many times in the past three and a half years?"

He snickered. "A dozen and a half, I'd reckon."

I turned my face into his chest. "How will I ever let go of my girls?"

He tightened his embrace. "You'll do it, dear. Just as you did today."

Could I send six beloved daughters into the world with all its dangers and allurements?

Somehow, I must.

A sudden realization struck, and I sat straight up. "What have I been thinking? I paraded alongside suffragists all across this country, fighting for exactly this—freedom for our girls. How can I expect them to remain tethered to my apron strings when they need to spread their wings and soar?"

Andrew laughed from his belly. "That's my Ella Jane. Good to have you back."

CHAPTER SIX

Therefore will we not fear, though the earth do change,
And though the mountains be shaken into the heart of the seas.
Psalm 46:2

The next two weeks of January wrapped around us like crisp sheeting, familiar but a bit chaffing.

"Wonder what Amy's doing today."

"Who's Grand Mama dragging her to meet?"

"How many soirees has she attended?"

"Where has she gone?"

"What has she done?"

Amaryllis's call the previous day had triggered my sense of foreboding. She'd complained of a sore throat and exhaustion. Her grandmother's personal physician had examined her, and Josephine had insisted she remain in Denver until whatever was ailing her had passed.

"I don't want to stay," Amaryllis had confided on the telephone.

"Aren't you too sick to travel, dear?"

"No, Mama. All I want is sleep."

Reluctantly, the Evanses booked Amaryllis first-class travel accommodations to Fair Valley.

As we boxed the holiday decorations, a litany of Bible verses about putting away fear lined up in my brain, but the girls' persistent queries kept me on edge. My anxiety wouldn't ease until I could examine my daughter myself.

I tried to set our thoughts on other subjects. "Have you girls packed for your return to CIA?"

Blossom shrugged. "Not much to do."

I wrapped a length of tree lights into a neat bundle. "Have all the photography supplies you need?"

She nodded.

"How about you, Camy?"

She folded a silver star in tissue paper. "Dresses laundered and ironed. Shoes cleaned and polished."

Dolly anticipated my question. "And books in a single crate."

I turned to the youngest two. "We're starting a unit on world religions this coming term."

"That means . . ." Ebony cocked her head. "Judaism—"

"Islam and Hinduism," Julia Jane added.

"Correct. Plus, we'll delve into a few more. Did you know, by the way, that Christianity is the only major religion whose founder claimed to be God?"

"Hmm." Ebony dropped her hands to her lap and fingered a sparkling angel. "Wouldn't it be exciting to visit the Middle East? Or India?"

Julia Jane perked up. "When Amy finishes college, she can go anywhere." She spread her arms wide. "Anywhere in the whole wide world."

I peaked one eyebrow. "Within reason, of course. But first, let's see how we can help your sister prepare for her final term at CIA."

The girls groaned.

"Don't tell us we have to launder her clothes."

"And iron them."

"Gather her books."

"And figure out which undies to pack. Ugh."

I raised both hands, palms exposed. "Would she do the same for you, my darlings?"

They glanced at one another and nodded.

"Finish up here, girls, while I work in the schoolhouse."

As I stepped outside, thunder grumbled overhead.

Andrew leaned out of his study door, and I was struck by the depth of color in his brown hair. "You and the girls stay in the house, dear. Could be a repeat of the lightning strike last August." He gazed at the boiling clouds. "I'll bring the well-bucket inside." The previous August, lightning had struck the copper pail on its way to the aquifer below.

I stuck my head inside the front doorway. "Your father fears another lightning strike, so stay in the house, girls." Upon their promises to do so, I ran toward the schoolhouse.

Our quirky pup Shaker scrambled down the mudroom steps and gamboled after me in his signature loose-legged manner. His every-which-way scruff resembled the black and white of salt and pepper from a shaker. The black fur surrounding both eyes like spectacles, often reminded me of all-seeing Providence.

Although we had enjoyed warmer than normal weather lately, a new front was mustering overhead, and temperatures would be dropping. Lightning danced in the distance.

I lit the school's two gas heaters, rummaged through a drawer for my reading glasses, and settled at my desk with Shaker lying beside me. "You don't have to keep track of your spectacles, do you, my boy?" He answered with an open-mouthed smile. Of sorts.

Pesky thoughts about my girls interfered with lesson preparation. When Dahlia had joined her elder sisters at CIA, their six-part chatter had been reduced to a duet. Still, their chiming voices ping-ponged in my memory. I released a deep sigh of gratitude.

When all six have flown the coop, what will Andrew and I do? No doubt I'll fill the schoolroom with other children. But will I be like Mama by then, frail and bent over with arthritis? Perish the thought.

A clap of thunder startled me to my feet. Andrew looked out a study window and ran to our porch. I closed up my lesson plans and joined him. Little Shaker followed, barking at the wind.

"A norther is on its way," Andrew said.

I shivered, recalling the damage such weather had wreaked on Oklahoma yearly. If we weren't enduring tornadoes like the one that had destroyed Mama's and Papa's place years ago, we were avoiding lightning like the strike last August. That one had shook the ground like a quake.

Julia Jane—with hair like Andrew's, as dark a brown as black-walnut shells—opened the door and stuck out her head. "We're getting scared. Ya'll coming in?"

"Sure, baby."

"Be right there."

While we laundered and packed the next day, a frigid wind rumbled in, and my spirits revived. I joined Andrew in our bed long before my usual midnight.

He drew me near. "What a pleasant surprise." The circle of warmth around him represented all things safe and loving. "Did you put up Shaker?"

"Sure did. I banked the fire in the family room. And checked the girls' radiators. I hope it isn't snowing when Amy arrives tomorrow."

"Don't borrow trouble, dear."

The sense of foreboding returned. "Trouble seems to follow lately."

On the day we'd agreed to make the Hanson girls our own, I'd vowed to expend my every breath on assuring their welfare.

In the process, I'd fallen more in love with them than I ever dreamed possible. I couldn't go on if anything happened to even one of them.

CHAPTER SEVEN

Make a joyful noise unto God, all the earth.
Psalm 66:1

I popped out of bed before the alarm sounded. Amaryllis was coming home today. We mustn't be late.
Apparently, the girls had awakened with the same thought. They tumbled downstairs, one scrambling past another as they had as children.

With my belly topsy-turvy, breakfast interested me not a whit. "Eat up, girls. Gotta keep up your strength. You've a long day ahead, plying Amy with questions. You'll wear yourselves out."

"Not like you, Mama." Dahlia spoke around a glob of oatmeal. "You'll be the last one in bed as usual."

Julia Jane pointed her fork from which dangled a string of scrambled egg. "You'll have a list of questions of your own, Mama."

"And so will you, Papa." Camellia mumbled as she broke apart a second biscuit and spread Nectar of Heaven, one of Mama's recipes. My girls claimed the syrupy, buttery concoction proceeded from where its name implied—heaven.

Andrew slurped his last bit of coffee and carried his dishes to the sink. "We can do the dishes when we return. Best set out soon. I see snow flurries."

I peered through the kitchen window. "Just as I feared."

He eased his hand around my waist. "No reason to fear, dear. Remember—"

I thumbed over my shoulder at the blackened Ebenezer on the mantel. "We're resting in the shadow of the Almighty."

He grinned and plastered a kiss on my cheek.

I wiped it away. "For heaven's sake, Andrew. I'll have to wash again."

His slippered feet all but skipped down our hallway.

The girls herded themselves up the stairs, and I listened for footsteps entering each room overhead. Our eldest's at the far end would provide the missing drumbeats tomorrow morning.

Bundled as we were with coats, ear and hand muffs, and the beaver furs Andrew had tanned in Colorado years ago, even the limousine's spacious interior strained at its seams. But it laughed at the slippery road to Fair Valley. We all did, I guess.

What a delight, my girls' mirth. I'd never grow tired of it.

Fair Valley's brick Main Street was icing over. The limousine slid one direction and another, but we arrived in one piece.

Andrew shifted into neutral. "I'll stay here with this contraption idling. Don't want to depend on it starting when we come back. I'll watch for the train."

"Well, I'm going inside. The stationmaster keeps the station toasty." I pushed open my door, crackling a thin layer of ice. "Wrap up good and tight, girls."

They joined me. With nothing but their eyes exposed, they resembled Eskimos in the photographs we'd perused in geography class.

"Hold hands, everyone. It's all for one, one for all."

In rubber-soled boots, we crept across the slippery ground, but the wind threatened to stall us. "Keep your heads down, girls!" Had the bluster carried my voice completely away?

Two of them nodded, and we plowed onward.

In the depot's warm interior, we stood beside the coal heater, warming our hands and dripping condensation.

"Waiting on the Denver train?" the stationmaster called to us.

"Yes. We are."

"Expect a delay. Got a cable a few minutes ago. Train crossed the Panhandle overnight and then came to a standstill. "

Oh no. "When do you expect it?"

He moved his head side to side. "Could be an hour or more."

The girls groaned, and I worried about the accumulating ice and snow between Fair Valley and Needham. And Andrew. Should he join us inside? He couldn't keep the engine idling for over an hour. I needed to alert him.

"Take your seats, girls." I pointed to the station seats against the interior wall. "Slip off your coats so you won't over-heat. That's a powerful stove. Could heat this little room faster than you expect. I'm going outside to talk with your papa."

"We'll stay right here."

"Won't even peek our noses outside."

"I'll keep an eye on the track yonder."

"So will I."

"Tell Papa to come inside. It's too cold out there."

"I agree with you." I tightened the muffler around my neck. "Be back in a minute."

The snow flurries had turned to blowing sleet that covered the wood planks like waxed linoleum. I took my time. It wouldn't do to fall and be on my back with Amaryllis just home. Plus, I'd be accompanying her sisters to Denton in two days.

I couldn't miss the luxury car. Steam poured out its stain-less-steel exhaust like a locomotive's. But I couldn't signal to

Andrew. The windows had fogged up. Fortunately, I made it to the front passenger door without a mishap.

"What's going on, Ella?" he said.

I'd expected he'd stay warm with the engine idling, but the interior felt as cold as the outside. I tugged down my muffler. "Train's delayed. By an hour or more. Hadn't you better come inside?"

He glanced at the fuel gauge. "If this behemoth sits in this kind of cold even an hour, I'm afraid it won't start. But the fuel level is dropping." He released a deep sigh. "Better come in." He killed the engine and met me at my door.

We locked arms. "Mighty slippery," he said.

"Just take it slowly."

The sleet blustered around us, but we managed to stay on our feet across the slippery ground and wooden planks leading to the depot. As we entered, the girls jumped to their feet.

"Papa."

"Amy's train was delayed."

"Got caught in ice and snow overnight."

"Yeah. In the Panhandle."

"Whatever that is."

"That's out west toward Beaver, girls." Andrew slipped off his outer coat and tossed his cap with ear flaps onto a chair. "Let me warm up."

I joined him at the stove, and the girls huddled around us.

Andrew looked to the stationmaster. "What's the latest word?"

"Last cable said they should pull up in another half hour. Their engine is burning a lot of coal about now."

I moved to the windows. Although the cold sent a chill through me, I felt closer to my absent daughter somehow. Watching the outside kept my anxious eyes busy.

The familiar three-part whistle drew the family to my side.

We bundled up, keeping our gazes glued to the tracks. When the obsidian-black engine pulled up and screeched to a standstill, expelling its exhaust like an overheated bull, we could contain ourselves no longer.

We ran outside, slipping and sliding but holding onto one another. The conductor wasted no time debarking the single Fair Valley passenger: our beautiful Amaryllis.

Tickled as a brood of finches in a pile of mash, we ran toward one another and huddled in a single mass.

"Mama, I don't feel good." Amaryllis's eyelids drooped.

"What's wrong, sweetheart?"

"Headache. Throat hurts. Weak as a kitten."

I examined her more closely. "You're looking peaked." Her skin was pale as ashes, but a pink spot shone on either cheek. I removed my gloves and slipped my hands under her muffler and along her neck. "I believe you have a little fever. Let's get you home and to bed."

CHAPTER EIGHT

My heart was hot within me
Psalm 39:3

Andrew arranged our daughter's belongings in the luggage rack. After he tinkered under the hood, the engine started. Blossom sat up front with her father, and I joined Amaryllis in the middle seat.

Amaryllis closed her eyes and leaned her forehead against the window glass. "Cold feels good. I could sleep a week, Mama."

"Overnight train travel can wear you out in the best of circumstances. But you aren't feeling well on top of it. We'll get you into bed right away."

With no more active sleet and the sun peeking through a gray cloud, ice on the roadway had softened, and the Pierce Arrow plowed right through.

Back at the cottage, the girls piled out and helped with the bags. Andrew sped away for Doc, and I helped my ailing daughter to a spare bedroom down our hall.

Blossom lit the fire while I turned down the bed and helped my young patient undress.

"Bring down a nightdress, Blossom."

"No flannel, Mama," Amaryllis croaked. "Too hot."

I covered her with a cotton sheet and laid my hands on her neck. "Can't let you get chilled either."

Blossom returned with a cotton chemise and an old, threadbare gown.

"Just chemise." Amaryllis's voice was growing hoarser, and she had begun to cough.

"Let's check your temperature first." In light of her persistent cough, I slid the mercury end under her arm. and she leaned backward onto the pillows. The five-minute wait, while my child's breathing and groaning increased, wound me tight as a pinwheel in a twister.

What in the world was taking Andrew so long? I focused on the wall clock. Surprisingly, only minutes had transpired. My nerves were showing. Removing the meter, I held it under the lamp light. One hundred-two degrees.

Setting the chemise and gown aside, I stood over the sick bed. "Let's see what we can do about that fever. You'll need to remain bare all over, but I'll guard your modesty, sweet one."

Setting a tray on the bedside table with a pitcher of water, bowl, isopropyl alcohol, and cloths, Blossom pointed to the pitcher. "That's cold well water, Mama."

I poured a glassful and raised my daughter for a sip through a paper julep straw.

She squinted one eye. "Tastes funny."

"Your taste buds are off, dear. Take more. It's good for you."

She submitted and emptied the glass.

I poured alcohol into the bowl and added a portion of cold water. Stirred. And soaked a thick cloth in the liquid. "I'll do your backside first, dear."

She groaned and rolled to her side.

I laid the wet cloth over her shoulders while a second soaked in the solution.

A tremor passed through her body. "So cold. And thirsty."

"Your sister's bringing more water." I spread the second cloth along her back and dipped the first into the alcohol mixture. Stunned at how quickly the cold liquid turned warm, I stifled a gasp. Mustn't alarm my sweet girl. "It's bringing your temperature down."

"Blossom," I called out the open doorway. "Bring another bowl and more water."

She and Camellia refreshed the alcohol solution while I continued the sponge bath. Amaryllis relaxed and fell into a deep sleep.

Andrew entered in a flurry of boot-heel tapping. "Doc's out of town. Called on him at his office and home. He's due back in a couple days. His nurse will call him in Tulsa."

"Meanwhile, bringing down Amy's fever is our priority. Please bring me aspirin, Blossom."

"And I'll go to the study and pray." Andrew zipped away as quickly as he'd entered.

Aspirin and an hour-long alcohol sponge bath brought down Amaryllis's temperature a degree. I slipped the drawstring chemise over her shoulders, pulled it down, and covered her with a sheet. "I'm going to your father. Sleep well. Be back soon."

She responded with a rumble in her chest and rolled to her side with her hands under her cheek. I fluttered the sheet, releasing a bit more warmth, and scrambled outside with Blossom keeping vigil at her sister's side.

"What do you think it is?" Pacing in Andrew's study, I'd twisted my hankie into a tight string.

"Mother's personal physician examined Amy. Said it's nothing but a sore throat and cough. Should be feeling better in a day or two." Andrew ran his fingers from his curved forelock to his crown. And back again.

"She picked up something in Denver, Andrew. I never

should've let her go." I plopped onto the divan and lowered my head to my hands.

He sat beside me. "Our girls have had sore throats and fevers over the years, dear. Surely this is more of the same. Try not to worry."

I lunged to my feet. "A mother not worry?"

"You know—"

"I know nothing but that my daughter is ill. And I won't rest until she's back to normal."

He sat staring out the window, no doubt mulling on me. And the Ebenezer inside.

Sometimes his faith screamed at me.

What now, Lord?

Only the wind answered. It whistled around the eaves and rattled the tin roof.

With Camellia watching over our invalid, I set out holiday leavings from the icebox, chipped slivers from the block of ice, and scooped them into a bowl. "Dolly, take this to Camy to cool the alcohol bath." I handed her a sprig of dried mint. "And add this to the pitcher of water."

I warmed chicken broth for the family, but we picked at our food. Ebony poured a portion into a wide-mouthed stone-ware mug, and I delivered it to our patient with a fresh pitcher of water with a sprig of dried mint. "Here, Amy. Take a bit of broth."

"Thirsty. Water," she replied in a strained voice.

I offered her another sip. "All this liquid will be going through you. But I have a commode ready."

She nodded. "Now."

"Up to getting out of bed? If not, I have a bedpan."

Her eyes closed, and her head lolled to the side.

Blossom scooted to the other side of the bed. "Here. I'll help."

The two of us completed the necessary task, and I returned to the cool compress.

Wringing out the cloth, I started with my daughter's feet. She made not a sound, didn't even a flinch, as I made my way up her legs and to her trunk. The cloth warmed quickly. I wrapped alcohol-soaked cloths around her ankles.

Andrew checked in intermittently and took over the vigil at two a.m. so I could sleep. The thermometer hovered at one hundred-one at first light.

"Maybe it'll go completely away today, dear one." My ever-optimistic husband poured himself a big glass of water and guzzled it down "Hmm. This from the well?"

"It is. Amy prefers it."

He sniffed the rim. "Is it just me, or does this water smell different?"

I checked it myself. "Smells like mint." I sniffed again. "Something might've fallen down the well. I'll tell Blossom to use the faucet water until you can examine the well."

CHAPTER NINE

Let thy tender mercies speedily meet us;
For we are brought very low.
Psalm 79:8

B lossom and Camellia beckoned to me from the hallway. "We're supposed to leave for Denton tomorrow," Blossom whispered atmy ear.

Camellia wrung her hands, and the space between her eyebrows puckered like a line of smocking.. "We're finishing our laundry this morning. But what do we do about Amy's?"

I nibbled on a thumbnail. "She's certainly not boarding that train."

The girls' expressions brightened. "Can we go alone this time?"

"Of course not. It isn't safe for you to travel that far without one of us. Either your father or I will accompany you." I paused to ruminate. "I'll arrange for an early morning departure and return to Fair Valley in the evening."

"That'll be hard on you." The corners of Camellia's mouth slid downward. "Can Papa tend her with one arm? Why doesn't he go with us and you stay with Amy?"

"Does Papa know what to do for her?" Forever the practical one, Blossom lifted both hands in a shrug. "And won't you need help yourself?"

"Your father insists. JJ and Ebony can help me for one day. And Doc will return home the next."

"When will she be able to travel?"

"Won't know for certain until Doc examines her. But I expect this won't last more than a few days. Add a day or two for recuperation, and she'll likely be no more than a week late this term. But I need to talk with the dean."

I'd been immersed in the suffrage movement until we women voted in 1920. During that time, the girls had developed strong opinions on the issues surrounding equality under the law. They each planned to lead lives on their own terms.

"Mama." Amaryllis's scratchy voice from the bedroom brought our conversation to a standstill.

"Coming, dear." I whispered *Please do Amy's laundry* to Blossom and Camellia, and they hurried toward the stairs.

"Thirsty, Mama."

I returned to my daughter's bedside and poured her a glass of mint- and lemon-flavored water, mulling on the well. The latest blustery weather had pitched deadfall down the shaft, but Andrew had removed it and found nothing serious amiss. Had he missed something?

A few teaspoonfuls of warm broth seemed to bring color into Amy's cheeks. Or was that a rash?

Our ministrations continued unabated, but by late afternoon, her temperature had risen to one hundred-three.

I gave her another sponge bath, and Blossom massaged her skin with cream.

Andrew returned not with his usual optimism but with worry sketched on his brow. "Did I hear you say her temperature's rising?" He laid his palm on her cheek. "Seems she should be improving by now, Ella. What else can we do?"

"Nothing I know. Not until Doc examines her."

He flopped into an armchair and rested his elbow on his knee. "I'll take over for you tonight."

"But—"

"No buts. I'm her father. I can sponge bathe her—face and neck, arms and hands, legs and feet—as well as you can. I refuse to leave her. That means tomorrow, too. You'll be traveling to Denton with the girls. I'm staying right here."

Truthfully, could I bear to leave my daughter in this condition, even for a day? But one of us needed to speak with the gentleman. I had met the gentleman on several occasions in the past, so perhaps I should be the one.

"All right, dear. But I wish you'd let me spell you tonight."

"No. I'm staying right here beside my girl."

What had come over mild-mannered Andrew? Was he blaming himself for Amy's illness? "Dear, please don't—"

"Papa?" Amaryllis had turned over. "You won't leave me, will you?"

He pulled his chair nearer and patted her cheek. "I won't. You can count on it, sweetheart."

I eased into the hallway with an urgent need for a bath and rest. But first, supper. Although none of us claimed an appetite, we emptied a pot of beans cooked with marrow bones and thick, crispy-on-the-outside cornbread. Thankfully, I was able to spoon bean juice between my daughter's lips.

Blossom joined me in the sick room after supper and sat to the side, weeping. "I don't want to leave for CIA without Amy."

"I know, dear, but—"

"Not going . . . without . . . me," Amaryllis croaked.

I leaned over her. "You're not well enough to travel tomorrow. I'll take you to Denton in a few days."

She twisted her head side to side. "No." A single, fat tear broke loose from her lashes and crept down her cheek. "Grad…"

"I'll speak with the dean, sweetheart. You might miss only a few days, but we'll see that you graduate with your classmates."

She brought her knees to her chest and folded into a ball. Her deep, moist sobs broke my heart. Andrew laid his head on her pillow and sobbed with her.

I sat back, fearing where this would end. *Please, Lord. Heal sweet Amy.*

When her sister fell asleep, Blossom stood. "I'm going to bed. Don't know how I'll sleep, though." She trudged out the door and plodded up the stairs.

Andrew and I moved our chairs to the window and watched the waning moon rise. Under present circumstances, we spoke not of ordinary things like our few cattle, my brood mare, or his Sunday sermon. Instead, we exchanged in hushed tones our concerns about storm clouds, lightning and thunder, and the explosions of the past world war, as if sparks from that conflagration's death and destruction could reach us now.

"I called Doc at his son's place in Tulsa."

I sat up, encouraged. "Is he coming right away?"

He rested his head in his hand. "Couldn't reach him. They might've traveled farther afield than Tulsa. I'll try again in the morning, love. And call Doc Barnard in Fair Valley if needed. Go on to bed. Tomorrow will be a big day for all three of you."

I trudged down the hallway to our room and lay in bed alone, staring at the beadboard ceiling and praying for God's mercy. Again.

CHAPTER TEN

And he remembered that they were but flesh,
A wind that passeth away, and cometh not again.
Psalm 78:39

B y morning, a mellow warm front had arrived. The thermometer on the back porch read forty-five degrees, and Amaryllis's temperature had lowered a degree.

Had the worst passed? If so, it may not necessary to bring in Doc Barnard. Andrew could decide.

I met Blossom, Camellia, and Dahlia in the hallway outside the sickroom.

"We've said our goodbyes to Ebony and JJ."

"How is Amy now?"

"Are you sure Papa can handle this alone?"

I enumerated my reply on my fingers and looked to each of them in turn. "Good. The same. And yes." I forced a big smile. "Now, it's heading toward fifty degrees. Let's take the Olds Torpedo."

"Mama." Amy had heard us and no doubt wanted to tell her sisters goodbye.

I slid into her room and motioned for the others to follow. "Don't get too close now. It might be catching."

The departing three threw kisses and backed into the hallway, silent as snowfall. Heartsick, I followed but forced a smile. The girls mustn't worry.

We drove to Fair Valley in the Torpedo, my gift from Andrew the previous year. Driving it brought back the memory of standing on our front porch and gawking at the cherry-red surprise.

"Do you like it?" Excitement and joy had lit Andrew's face.

"What is it and what's it doing in our driveway?"

"It's yours."

I looked him straight in the eyes. "Have you gone mad? Why?"

"No need to drive that limousine for errands and ladies' gatherings."

"How did you pay for it?"

He shrugged. "Sold some stock. Outlook for the market in coming years isn't good, so I got rid of some shares now."

I was stunned speechless.

"Say something, love."

"Seems like a dream."

"No dream. It's an Oldsmobile Torpedo, and it's for real. Let's go for a ride."

I never shall forget the joy of that excursion, a golden moment in time—the engine putt-putting, Andrew working the gears, and me holding on to my hat.

Today, the contraption suited my three college-bound girls and me. Meanwhile, their younger sisters would see that their father had what he needed for his patient.

Wrapped in lightweight woolen headgear, we rode with the top down to enjoy the close-to-perfect day. The gently rolling landscape—part fallow and part speckled by grazing cows and horses—met the eastern horizon like old friends. The soft breeze had set windmills to spinning, reminding me of spring's first wildflower crop—cheerful, welcoming, and not afraid to stand out.

But it wasn't spring. It was winter, and as long as my daughter lay abed, it would remain so.

At the Fair Valley station, we parked, and a porter welcomed us with a tip of his cap. He loaded our luggage onto a flat-bed cart, and we women pulled up our auto's collapsible top and locked it into place.

We brushed dust off our hands and aimed for the depot arm in arm.

Blossom's shoulders sagged forward as she walked. "What if Amy gets worse while you're gone? Can Papa and the girls handle it?"

"I'm sure they can. Besides, Doc should be back in town anytime."

"When you return, you'll call us if anything changes, won't you?"

I patted Camellia's hand on my arm. "You know I will, dear one."

Dahlia brought us to a halt. "You won't forget? Promise us."

Smiling at them in turn, I gestured forward. "I promise." How wonderful it would be to call them with good news when I returned. The alternative didn't bear considering.

I purchased our tickets from the stationmaster, and we settled in the passenger waiting area. The girls fidgeted, and I took to my feet and paced.

Commotion at the door drew my eyes. A handsome, black-haired young man held open the door for a female traveler to enter. Adjusting her hat, the woman's head was lowered, and when she looked up, I stared, stunned.

My sister Viola and her son Joshua?

I gasped and ran toward them. "Look at you, Joshua. You're all but grown. What are you doing here, Vi?" She and I had been estranged for a time, but we had reunited in a fashion years ago. Our subsequent visits at Mama's had been strained, but unexpectedly finding her standing before me erased time, circumstance, and every speck of discord. But as I wrapped my arms around both of them, dark memories flashed, prickling my midsection.

Before Andrew and I married, Frank Irving, my jealous, mean-spirited former suitor, had instigated an argument with Andrew at a cotton gin. The altercation escalated, and Andrew fell into the gin's savage blades, mangling my beloved's left arm.

Afterwards, willful Viola had married the scheming ne'er-do-well, and while he was imprisoned, she had moved with their son to McAlester where they could visit Frank

Appearing as stunned as I, she paused, as if words failed her. "Why, we're here to meet Frank."

I flinched. "Frank? How in the world—"

"He was granted clemency, and he's coming home a dozen years earlier than expected."

My mouth eased open. "Frank's coming home from prison?"

She nodded with a wide grin. "Today."

The news held me stock-still. The man who had attempted to steal my innocence two decades ago, the criminal responsible for my husband's maiming, the scoundrel who had eloped with my rebellious sister, was arriving at this depot today?

Heaven forbid Frank and I come face to face, not with the recent anguish that had descended on our household and with my daughters watching my every move. My girls knew the circumstances behind their uncle's imprisonment, but they hadn't met my Viola and Joshua. And they certainly didn't know about Frank's attack on my virtue.

Viola gasped and held out her arms. "Don't tell me these are three of your girls. Why, they're grown." My threesome stood with startled expressions as she grabbed them in an earnest embrace. She held them at arm's length. "Just look at you. Why,

you're grown. Mama said four of your girls were in college."
She tapped her bottom lip and then pointed to them. "Let's see
. . . you're Amaryllis. You're Blossom. And . . ."

The girls shook their heads and pointed to themselves.

"I'm Blossom."

"I'm Camellia."

"And I'm Dahlia."

My beauteous sister scanned the room. "Where's everybody
else?"

I took a deep breath and exhaled through pursed lips.
"Amy's at home under the weather. And the other two are with
Andrew."

"I'm sorry I'll miss them. We've just moved into the Irvings'
old home. Haven't even told Mama and Papa yet."

Frank Irving would be living just across the road from us.
Horrors.

"We'll be able to visit often." She offered the idea as if it
were a grand bit of news.

Without Frank. Please.

Joshua cleared his throat, startling me around. "For goodness sakes. I've taken leave of my good sense. How handsome
you've grown. Why, you're a man now." About Dahlia's age,
he was as handsome as I had expected and stood taller than his
mother. His black hair and eyes mimicked his father's, but where
Frank's gaze chilled, Joshua's was a breath of warm summer
breeze.

He grinned and nodded. "Almost, Aunt Ella. In my first
year of college.

"Good for you. Amy's in her last term at CIA. We'll be
attending the other girls' graduations each May for the next five
years."

A southbound train squealed to a standstill, and we all
whipped around to stare.

"This is your father's train." Viola urged her son out the door.

We stood at the plate-glass window and observed a much older Frank, drawn and thin, step from the train into his wife's and son's embraces.

She pulled him inside the waiting area, pointing at me and the girls. Had she no sense at all?

"Can you believe it, Frank? It's Ella and three of her girls. Aren't they beautiful?"

Our encounter proved to be as awkward as I had feared. Eventually, our magpie Viola stopped chattering with a start, as if she'd become aware of her surroundings and our strained expressions. She mumbled a few words about getting her husband home, and the three of them whisked away.

My girls plied me for explanations about my sister's and nephew's odd absence from our lives. But I told them we'd talk about it later. It was a tale that would take time to spin.

Truthfully, I found speaking Frank's name akin to forcing down a slug of Black Draught—almost more than I could swallow.

CHAPTER ELEVEN

Hath God forgotten to be gracious?
Hath he in anger shut up his tender mercies?
Psalm 77:9

B etween visits with CIA's dean and medical staff, I called Andrew several times. Amaryllis's temperature remained the same. But vomiting and diarrhea now plagued her.

I stepped off the train in Fair Valley well after sunset, dreading the hour-long trip to Needham, alone in the darkness. When I pulled into our circular driveway and lowered the foot brake, a lone light shone through a single window. Andrew was tending our daughter.

I found him asleep at her side, holding her hand. I nudged him. "How's she doing, dear?"

Startled awake, his eyes bloodshot and bleary, he scrubbed his face with his hand. "Her temperature went back up around nightfall, and I bathed her as well as I could. But then vomiting and diarrhea came on like a firestorm."

"Get some sleep. I can take over."

"I'll rest awhile, but not for long. You and I can tend her together."

I ran my fingers through his hair and patted his drooping forelock into place. "The girls are fast asleep, I take it."

He nodded. "Camy took word to your parents. Asked them to pray." He staggered toward our suite down the hall.

Pushing the chair aside, I leaned over my daughter. As pale as a winter rose, her skin appeared translucent and her chest rose and fell in shallow breaths. I ran my hand along her neck. She was on fire.

I slipped the thermometer under her arm and stepped back to wait. Sponge bath supplies sat on the bedside table where Andrew had left them. Throwing off her sheet and thin blanket, I bathed her from her feet to her neckline, this time with undiluted alcohol. She moaned and stirred a bit but fell into a fitful sleep, shivering and with teeth chattering.

Covering her as I moved up her body, I discovered a homemade diaper of sorts made from a small towel. She was emaciated, and the sight of her belly startled me. Slightly distended, it was covered in red, uneven spots.

Did Amaryllis have measles?

The thermometer registered one hundred-four degrees.

I spread Calamine lotion on the rash and covered her with the sheet. And prayed.

Do something. Please.

A car engine puttered in the driveway around midnight. I peeked out. Looked to be Doc.

He let himself in. "Where's everyone?" he called from the entry.

"Down here."

He rushed into the room. "Just got the word today. We'd gone to Fort Smith. What's going on?"

"Her temperature's one-o-four now. Vomiting and diarrhea. And there are red spots on her trunk."

He slipped her gown aside. "Abdomen's swollen too." He pressed against the distention.

She moaned and flung her head side to side, mumbling incoherently.

"How long's she been like this?"

I recounted the details of the past few days.

"Has she been around anyone who's sick?"

"Not here. But who knows about Denver? Her grandmother kept her busy making social calls."

He scratched his head. "You have town water, don't you?"

I nodded. "We tap into Addie's line."

He studied the floor and rubbed a forefinger and thumb over his chin. "Ever use your old well?"

"Every now and then. Amy prefers the water."

"How far is it from the outhouse?"

I shrugged.

"About twenty feet." Andrew had appeared suddenly with his hair standing on end.

I reached for his hand.

Doc muttered to himself. "Has she drunk from the well recently?"

I felt a line crawling like an etching tool along the space between my eyebrows. "She's had some since she returned home."

"No. Would've had to be earlier, like before she left for Denver."

Andrew and I agreed we would have no way of knowing.

And then I recalled. "She prefers well water for bathing. Says it leaves her skin silkier. She took a deep swig before she bathed on New Year's Day. Now that I think about it, she commented that it tasted funny."

Doc *humphed* and pulled two glass tubes and a syringe from his bag. "I'll collect blood and urine samples and leave for Oklahoma City immediately. Since she's been sick more than a week, I'll insist on the test results in twenty-four hours and return as quick as I can."

"What do you think this is, Doc?"

He collected the samples and dropped them into his bag.

Snapping the latch closed, he turned to us with a deep huff. "I'd bet my license on this being typhoid fever."

Andrew and I gasped, and our hands squeezed tight.

"Initial symptoms are like other conditions—weakness or fatigue, headache, sore throat, and rising temperature. Unlike less serious conditions, however, the symptoms intensify after a week. The headache becomes severe; temperature rises to one hundred-four and -five; and there's abdominal pain, vomiting, and possible diarrhea.

"The bacteria are transmitted through direct contact with an infected person or by ingesting contaminated food or water." He looked toward the back door. "The old privy being so close to the well worries me."

Andrew slumped forward and wailed. "It's my fault."

"Why?" Doc asked.

"Before we tapped into Addie's water line, the water table dropped so low during the drought that by '18 we had to have the well dug deeper. Found underground shifting that could've affected the stability of the soil beneath the old outhouse. When rains came, the contents of the old cesspool would've risen to the surface through fissures."

I snapped my fingers. "Lightning struck around the well not long ago."

"Could've created a fissure," Doc said, "and the cesspool could've leaked into your water supply. I'll send in a sample, but in the meantime, use faucet water. Boil sheets, towels, and other cloth items that've come into contact with Amy over the past two weeks. Disinfect everything—all hard surfaces and the floor with a good lye solution. Do you have an unopened container of commercial lye on hand?"

"I do."

"Dissolve one pound in five and a half gallons of pure water. Wipe everything off with heavy gloves with no tears or holes in them. Keep things disinfected with an ordinary chlorinated lime solution afterwards.

"I must report my suspicions to the county health department. If the test comes back positive, they'll quarantine you and your girls here in the house for two weeks. Has anyone in your family had typhoid?"

"No. None of us have had it."

He scratched his scalp. "And Oklahoma's supply of vaccine hasn't reached this far into the countryside yet."

"What can we do now?"

Doc provided instructions on Amaryllis's care and guarding against the infection ourselves. When he left, Andrew and I followed along behind him like a pair of bedraggled puppies. Watching him drive away, the weakness of sheer terror overcame us, and we fell against one another, weeping bitter tears.

CHAPTER TWELVE

I am weary with my groaning;
Every night make I my bed to swim;
I water my couch with my tears.
Psalm 6:6

Andrew wiped his daughter with cool cloths through the wee hours of the morning, and I prepared the house according to Doc's instructions. Meanwhile, her vomiting became retching, and her moaning turned to plaintive cries.

Unceasingly, it seemed, she flailed and rolled into a ball, groaning. "Make it go away, Papa."

"You'll be better soon, love. Try to sleep."

Have mercy, Lord.

Viola knocked at dawn. "Like you, I've had typhoid, so I'm staying here to help." She raised a manicured finger of caution. "Frank and Joshua can take care of themselves."

Doc returned midmorning with test results. "It's typhoid fever. I'm sorry."

Andrew and I stared at the man with our mouths ajar.

"But I was able to round up an experimental antitoxin. Won't hurt to give it a try." He pulled a dark-brown bottle from his bag and administered the liquid with its eyedropper. Her lips puckered, and she sputtered.

When she settled, Doc ushered us into the hallway. "You

both need rest. I've procured the services of a nurse. She'll be here anytime now. I'll stay until she arrives."

"I can't let my girl—"

"Your girl needs you healthy, Andrew. Both of you." He turned us toward our bedroom. "Do as I say. We'll take care of Amy."

We dragged ourselves into our bedroom. Clear, crisp January tossed sun rays through the stained glass above our bed. A blackthorn tree stretched across the glass canvas, showering an array of colors across the room. We washed up and changed into bedclothes and toppled into the loving warmth of our bed.

My husband gathered me to him, and I crumbled against his chest. "How can this be happening? The Lord has forsaken us."

He tightened his hold around my middle. "Quite the opposite. He provided this home as a shelter."

"Shelter? Certainly not from death. Case in point, three sons buried outside and Amy in this condition."

"Some folks live unscathed by tragedy. Others have known little else."

"But why?"

"Beyond our understanding. Gotta leave such quandaries in God's hands and trust Him."

I squirmed at his side. "You've been mulling on this, haven't you?"

"Been praying of course. But prayer goes both ways, so I've done some listening too. Mind if I share a bit?"

I nodded against his chest.

"For sixteen years now, we've been living in this house amid warmth that has nothing to do with the flames in the fireboxes and everything to do with God's hand of blessing. The spirit in this home comes from our love not only as family but as children of God."

I sniffled. "But our family's been decimated."

"Hardly, dear. We have six beautiful, intelligent, strong-spirited daughters. Our sons lived and died here. They weren't with us long, but they stitched their fingerprints on our hearts, and we'll carry them always.

"The Lord's the One who'll make the stitches hold. Just leaving the past behind and stumbling through the days ahead isn't all He's asking of us. He wants us to go *toward* tomorrow and all the days after that, with purpose, into the future where He is, trusting His love every step of the way."

The wheels in my brain turned in time with the thumping of Andrew's heart.

"The pain we've endured has been excruciating, we both know. I looked up that word and, of all things, found the cross."

"What do you mean?" My voice was hoarse and trembly.

"Excruciating means 'out of the cross.' God witnessed the excruciating death of His child. We have something in common with Him. We know the meaning of the word in ways other folks never will. I believe He expects us to do something worthwhile with that knowledge. Let's you and I stand on His promise to be the rock that's higher than our troubles."

The following week consisted of a merciless nightmare.

The antitoxin had no effect.

Dear Amaryllis's temperature rose to one hundred-five degrees. She went into convulsions, and Doc ordered ice packs.

Then came delirium. We had to hold her in her bed at those times.

Terror consumed me, bringing on aberrations of my own. "The mad dog has a hold of Amy. Do something, Andrew!"

"That dog isn't anywhere around, dear."

"He's tearing her apart! Look at her!"

"That dog's dead, dear."

"Bring me the ebony. Quick!"

The nurse restrained me, and Doc gave me a sedative.

Poor Andrew could only watch and pray.

I slept through one day. Waking with a clear head, I rushed to my sick child. "How is she?"

"'Bout the same." Andrew spoke in a flat, emotionless tone.

"You must rest too."

"It's my fault. If only when . . ."

"You couldn't know something like this would come of that drought."

"Should've stayed on it. Asked questions. Had the water tested. Watched the old site closer. Something."

I wrapped Amaryllis's gentle warrior in my arms. "Only God has the sort of knowledge you're expecting of yourself. You've said that more times than I can count."

"I should've . . ." He disintegrated into a million pain drenched pieces of manhood.

We could only hold on to one another and cry out to our Maker.

In the third week, the delirium passed. Our child lay motionless with her eyes half closed. Her distended abdomen rose and fell with each labored breath.

"Doc, can't somebody do something?" Andrew pleaded. "Look at her. Not an ounce of strength left in her."

"This is the typhoid state. If she can make it through this and not hemorrhage internally, she may live."

Intestinal bleeding began the next day.

Andrew was inconsolable. "It's my fault. Dear God, it's my fault."

"Amy's prognosis isn't good," Doc said. "You must prepare yourselves for the worst. I'm very sorry. Blood banks were developed during the Great War and are maintained in large hospitals today. The closest is Oklahoma City. I placed an order by phone, but . . ."

"But what?" Andrew and I spoke in frantic unison.

"If she develops sepsis—blood poisoning—that will negate any good a transfusion will do. If that happens, Amy's chances of survival are very poor indeed. I'm so very sorry to be the bearer of such sad news."

We called the girls and broke the news, and they returned home on the next train.

Meanwhile, Doc administered a transfusion but diagnosed sepsis on the twenty-eighth day.

Then her liver and kidneys failed.

Andrew couldn't sleep and wouldn't eat. In a place beyond the reach of mortals, he breathed, but that was about all. My touch and words meant nothing.

Our sweet daughter's brave heart stopped beating on January 31, a full sixteen years after she first walked through our front door.

Andrew collapsed onto the floor.

I sat beside him with his head in my lap and watched my tears mingle with his.

The nurse stooped to help us, but I pushed her away. "Take your hands off me! Don't touch my husband. Leave us be."

She stepped into the hallway, and the door clicked shut.

Panic resided in the past.

Frenzy had halted.

Our lovely Amaryllis slept.

Thunder rumbled low overhead. Raindrops pinged and pounded, spotting the windowpanes. .

I pointed to the window. "Heaven's bawling."

He whisked his hand over his eyes. "But Amy's at peace."

How would I tell the other girls? How would we all face life without Amaryllis?

Doc returned and pulled a chair beside us. "I need to contact the funeral director. Rest awhile."

We called the girls downstairs and delivered the dreadful news. Inconsolable, they collapsed beside us, the seven of us sharing one another's sorrow.

Andrew called his parents in Denver, and Josephine insisted on setting the funeral no sooner than a week. "I couldn't possibly prepare in less time."

With the girls settled in their beds upstairs, Andrew and I leaned on one another and plodded toward our bedroom, crumbling into our bed.

"Lord, please hear our cry," Andrew murmured out of the blue. "You're our only hope. You've gone ahead with outstretched wings. Teach us to trust you."

The gentle rain and distant rumbles lulled us, and we slept in one another's arms.

CHAPTER THIRTEEN

He brought me up also out of a horrible pit, out of the miry clay;
And he set my feet upon a rock, and established my goings.
Psalm 40:2

W e buried Amaryllis beside her brothers on the seventh
of February.

The ground was still soft from recent rains. A norther
had blown in the night before, and our world turned into a
bluster with a bite.

Owen supported Andrew.

Mama and Papa held on to each other.

And I leaned on my five girls.

A bitter wind flung bits of debris into my face, biting and
stinging.

My thoughts mirrored the wind's bitterness. *So, Andrew,
where's your Ebenezer now?*

The walk home from the cemetery took on the cadence of
a death march. Our shoes drummed a rhythm tailor-made for
dying. *Time-to-die. Time-to-die. Time-to-die.*

In the house, I covered my ears to muffle the ghastly sing-
song, but it rattled through the floorboards into my feet. My
body vibrated to the rhythm of the dirge.

Viola wrapped an arm around my shoulders. "I'll stay a
few more days."

"What would I do without you, sis?" What a change. There was a time when the two of us couldn't bear to sit in the same room together.

Darkness I couldn't name seemed to descend. Even with Andrew beside me, I could only bend forward, clutch my middle, and groan. Prayer was out of the question; I couldn't line up words so they made sense.

Andrew's prayers over me, and Mama's and Papa's, rose to the sky and hung like smoke.

"She's set out on a journey of grief," Doc whispered to Andrew. . "But she'll come around with proper medication and loving care."

Made no difference to me. I was as weak as a loose ball of yarn. How could I wake each morning knowing my daughter wasn't with us and never would be again? How could I pass her closed door the rest of my days?

"Leave me to the miry pit, for heaven's sakes, Andrew. And get rid of that cursed Ebenezer. Sign of protection, my foot."

Bright, beautiful Amaryllis had glided into our life sixteen years, one month, and seven days ago. She had graced us with joy, curiosity, hope, and love. And then she had glided away.

No more delirium. Fevered eyes. Or tears on her sunken cheeks.

No more pleas for relief.

No more Amaryllis.

Owen and Josephine withdrew to their suite at Needham Hotel.

In Dahlia's room, we seven bunched on the floor in a heap of damp curls and cotton nighties. They smelled of lilac and lavender. We cooed our love and devotion, and they sighed and purred back. They wept and asked why Amy'd had to go. Neither of us had a decent answer.

"I don't know," Andrew said at length. "That's the truth, plain and simple. One day we'll understand. Until then, let's love on one another and thank God we can."

That evening, he spent time alone in his study. I caught glimpses of him hunkered over his desk, writing. When he came to bed, I examined his pallor. "You look pale, love."

"Sorrow saps every ounce of strength from a body."

"Sleep'll help us both."

We took to our bed, and the girls gathered around us. "Remember when you read to us when we were little?" Dahlia said.

"Of course," we responded.

Julia Jane held out a Bible, and Andrew read the passage about the resurrection of Lazarus.

Dahlia asked if she'd see Amy again, and Andrew assured her she would.

Blossom steered her sisters back upstairs, and we stared at empty space.

Andrew leaned back and closed his eyes. "I'm hot."

I laid my hand on his forehead, cheeks, and neck. "You *are* hot."

"Can't make out if it's a fevered spirit or something else. Haven't felt good for a couple of days. Weak."

Tell me this isn't Amy all over again.

"Don't worry, Ella. We've been through a storm. I'll be better in the morning."

I made up a cot at the foot of our bed, but sleep proved elusive.

Our final nightmare began the next morning with Andrew gagging. "Hot . . . head . . . throat . . ."

I pulled out the thermometer and took a reading. "One hundred-three. I'll call Doc."

He knocked right away and signaled me to join him in the

hallway. "Could be a passing bug. Or stress and grief have pulled him down."

"Think it's typhoid?"

He scratched his head. "First symptoms can take as long as three weeks to appear. When he tended Amy, did he disinfect properly?"

"Said he did, but I wasn't beside him all the time. Found him all but curled up alongside her a time or two." I paused as a finger of ice poked my midsection. "And he drank a whole glass of well water the day Amy returned from Denver."

"Gotta be honest with you. I fear he's contracted typhoid."

I struggled for a breath, wheezed. Coughed.

Doc leaned me backward with my head tilted onto the chair back. "There now, Ella. You're alright. Relax. Take a deep breath."

My lungs expanded, and with a gasp came welcome relief.

The nurse took up residence again, and I sat vigil at Andrew's side.

Turned out, no Widal test was required. Andrew's illness took much the same course. Fever of one hundred-three, diarrhea, and vomiting the first week.

His parents hovered at our house each day but avoided the sickroom as Doc directed. Josephine instructed the girls in the foolishness of building a "dreadfully backward country life devoid of proper medical care."

The church ladies delivered three meals each day.

When Mama and Papa stopped by, they brought comfort and a sense of security.

"Here's boiled chicken and noodles." Mama set the covered bowl on the counter.

Papa nodded. "Enough for all six of you. And thin broth for Andrew."

I hugged them both close. "Thank you. Will you stay?"

"Only to clean up." Mama grabbed a dish towel, and Papa found the broom.

Andrew woke me before dawn the next morning. "Ella?"

"Yes?"

"Can't stop thinking about what I should've done to take care of the well. If only . . ."

"You couldn't've known what was happening underground, dear."

"Now I'm tied to this bed, and you're nursing me. You haven't stopped to grieve."

"I have the rest of my life to grieve, Andrew. Right now, I want you well."

He moaned and rolled to his side. "My spirit's weak. Bring me the Ebenezer, please."

Sitting up, I tugged my fingers through my hair, an unruly mass of curls. "Don't know what you want with that old thing. Makes my skin crawl."

Back in the living room, I forced myself to lift the dreadful limb from the mantel. Shuddering at the memories it unearthed and disgusted at its unfulfilled promise of shelter under the wings of the Almighty, I set it above our bedroom fireplace.

"Put it over here near me."

I moved it to our dresser, and he relaxed. He claimed the old Ebenezer brought him comfort, but it chilled my gut.

Andrew dropped off to sleep, and I slogged down the hall toward the kitchen. Time to face another day.

The second week, Andrew's temperature hovered at one hundred-four degrees, and delirium set in, bringing to mind my former hallucinations

"Watch out for the lightning, Ella!"

"It's clear outside, dear."

"Get away from that well!"

"We're safe and sound in our home, love."

I bathed him with cold cloths soaked in alcohol.

CIA granted the girls permission to postpone their studies until summer.

Viola moved back in upstairs. When my legs and spirit gave out, knowing she was tending my girls strengthened me. When I stood by Andrew and wiped his brow, knowing my sister was feeding my girls fed my spirit. When I watched the nurse's frenzied movements, picturing Viola calming my girls with kind explanations calmed my soul. And when I prayed for an end to Andrew's suffering, I knew my sister was praying with my beloved children. Her unexpected, sweet ministrations bolstered me.

Where was that willful, jealous sibling of yesteryear? We hadn't been able to talk about her years in McAlester, keeping vigil over her own husband. Someday . . .

Andrew's delirium increased in the third week. And then came stupor.

Through the three weeks of tending him, I'd forced myself to pray what he had prayed over our sweet daughter. *Please shelter us in the shadow of your wings.* Unendingly.

Had it been pointless?

CHAPTER FOURTEEN

But my lovingkindness will I not utterly take from him,
Nor suffer my faithfulness to fail.
Psalm 89:33

At the beginning of the fourth week, Doc looked at me with something other than pure fear. "With little internal bleeding, looks like he'll make it."

"Thank you, God." Tears of joy left me weak.

Doc helped me to a chair. "He's tolerated clear liquids. But this must continue until I tell you otherwise." He held me by my shoulders and peered straight into my eyes. "Listen well. He'll beg you for solid food, but you mustn't be swayed. He could hemorrhage. Do you understand?"

I nodded and laid my head on his aged shoulder. "You've done so much for us, Doc. How can I thank you?"

"Take care of Andrew. That's thanks enough. And don't forget to disinfect."

Relieved and thankful for the encouraging report but brimming over with sorrow over Amaryllis, I ambled toward Rock Creek and found it singing.

Papa found me standing with my arms crossed over my middle. "Sit down, daughter. Let's talk. I can see you're as skittish as a filly in her first snow."

When I sat, the tears started. Papa just held me. My heart was too full of pain to speak.

I had to leave the spigot open until it ran dry. Then I could take in fresh air and figure out what needed saying.

Papa broke the silence. "The past year's been a mighty trial for you and Andrew. Breaks my heart. What can I do to help?"

"It's God, Papa."

"Why God?"

"I can't trust Him anymore."

Papa waited to speak. Knowing him, he was chewing on my words and figuring how to answer. "What do you mean exactly?"

"If God can't be trusted to take care of a man as good as Andrew, He can't be trusted at all."

Papa knew better than to answer before thinking first, so I waited.

"Our Heavenly Father causes it to rain on the just and the unjust," he said at length. "Jesus taught that in the Sermon on the Mount."

"What's the point in being one of the just then?"

"It makes a mighty difference, Ella. The blood of Jesus makes us just, so our lives must glorify Him, not ourselves. Even when we hurt and don't understand. You know that."

"But why such a flood of suffering?"

"God sends rain as a flood at times. Other times He sends no rain a'tall, but He grows His young'uns either way. The Apostle Paul told the persecuted Christians in Rome that suffering produces character. It brings God's loved ones closer to him. Isn't growing closer to God the goal of every one of us?"

"Sure. But you'd think a God of love would spare His own children such sorrow and trials." I'd expressed the same utter disappointment with God when Andrew had suffered his accident sixteen years ago. And when my children died.

"That's the way His children think, but since He's God and we aren't. I expect there's a heap we never will understand. Gotta trust him until we look him in the face."

"That's what Andrew said when our children died."

"He was right, you know."

"But how do I learn to trust Him?"

"Keep praying. And remember when loved ones tend you, He's feeding you manna from heaven." Papa talked on about God's faithfulness and love while the stream serenaded us.

"You think Andrew's accident and my children's deaths are rocks in the creek bed of my life, don't you?"

"Sure as the world."

"How do I sing when I hurt so badly?"

"You can't, but Jesus *in* you can. If you keep running to him, before you know it, you'll be singing like this brook."

"Will you pray for me to turn this hurt into a song?"

"I already do, dear one. Every day."

At the fork in the trail, Papa took the path westward toward his farm, and I aimed southward to the cottage. Owen and Josephine were due to visit.

I found them in the living room and motioned them to follow. "Andrew's still abed, but

Doc says he's doing better."

Owen took my hand and slipped it through the crook of his arm. "You're nothing short of a gift from God."

Acutely aware of his tower-straight wife beside me, I patted his hand. "So are you. I know where Andrew got his tender heart."

Josephine *tsk-tsked* and entered the sickroom.

"Your parents are here," I whispered to Andrew.

"Mother? Father?"

She rushed to his bedside. "Yes, my darling son! Your mother's here."

"Father?"

"I'm here, son." Owen stood in the doorway.

"I couldn't wait another moment," his mother said. "I've been in torment, wondering and waiting. Oh, the agony!" She sniffled. "I've come to take you home. Tomorrow. We'll see that you receive the right kind of care. I've made all the arrangements."

"I *am* home."

"Of course, darling. I meant home with me." She dabbed her face with a lace-trimmed handkerchief.

"My home . . . with Ella."

Aiming to ease the discomfort of the moment, I looked to Owen. "Please have a seat at the fireplace."

"We need time with our son," Josephine barked.

"All right. I'll leave you alone then."

As I left the room, Owen embraced me. "Thank you for your loving care of our son. He wouldn't live without you."

"Nor I without him. I love you, Owen."

"Mother . . . starving." As I stepped into the hallway, Andrew's request stopped me in my tracks.

"I'll see that you're fed. What would you like?"

"Ham . . . red eye gravy."

"Maybe in a few days." I tossed the reply over my shoulder.

Josephine's fine silk skirt rustled. "Don't worry, son. Mother's here."

I busied myself in the kitchen and spent the day tending the house. Energy born of pent-up fury meant the cottage would shine come sundown.

I met Josephine in the kitchen at suppertime. "You mustn't give Andrew solid food. He could hemorrhage if he gets more than his insides can tolerate."

"He can die of starvation too. He's nothing but skin and

bones!" Her eyes flashed with a fire that brought thunderstorms to mind.

"He'll not expire of starvation with the clear liquid diet Doc prescribed."

"What does a simple country doctor know? My son needs food. If his wife won't feed him, his mother will."

With my ire rivaling the stove's rising heat, I pointed straight at her nose. "I forbid it. If that means I bar you from the door, so be it."

"Whoa, dear ones." Owen entered the kitchen and placed a hand on each of our shoulders. His touch stilled my racing heart. "Shouting will do nothing to improve Andrew's condition. Let's talk about this like sensible Christians ought."

I explained as best I could. "Doc Butler says no solid food yet. That's the end of it."

He turned to his wife. "Do you understand?"

She huffed and crossed her arms over her chest.

"When the time comes, you can feed him if you like, Josephine," I said.

"I'll do that, you can be sure." She punctuated her statement with a firm nod and pranced out.

Lord, help. She's a two-year-old JJ.

Ravenous for solid food over the next few days, Andrew continued to pester. "I'm starving."

"Can't. Doc's orders."

"Can't live like this."

"No, but solid food would kill you."

His pleas haunted me. I longed to see a healthy glow replace the sickly pallor, but I couldn't feed him. I simply couldn't.

I sat at his bedside and read his Sunday lessons and Scripture aloud. Hearing God's words strengthened his spirit. It confirmed to me that he belonged in the pulpit, the center of God's will.

CHAPTER FIFTEEN

But I trusted in thee, O Jehovah:
I said, Thou art my God.
Psalm 31:14

A warm front descended on the seventh of March, and Mama and Papa helped me open the windows.

Josephine and Owen showed up at our bedroom door on that warm and muggy day. Gussied up in finely woven and embroidered broadcloth, she settled into the rocker beside her son.

"I've brought knitting." She held up a basket.

"I was just putting dinner on the table. Care to join us?"

"I'll eat later, but you go on, Owen."

I pointed to a bowl of broth on the bedside table. "You can feed Andrew."

She jerked her head in a nod. "I'll do that." As she spooned broth into her son's mouth, her lined lips tightened in a firm line.

"I'd like to take the girls to town," Owen said. "You too if you'd like. Can't think of a better way to use our rented Cadillac."

"I'd appreciate that. It's the first Tuesday of the month, the day for the farmer's market. Thank you for thinking of me."

"It was my idea," Josephine said. "Takes a woman to anticipate a woman's needs."

"Then I thank you too." That woman beat all I ever saw. When she stepped into my house, I drew into a mass of knotted nerves. Bless Owen.

Owen joined the girls and me in the kitchen. We fixed plates and took them to the porch. Papa visited with Owen while we ate, and Mama lingered in the kitchen.

I peeked in and found her cleaning up. "You're in no shape to be doing dishes, Mama. The girls can do that."

She steadied herself on the cabinet and winced. "Leave me be, daughter mine."

When our utensils stilled, Mama called us inside. "Run along now. Have a good time at the market." She flung a dish towel over a hook and signaled Papa toward the back.

"Going to the store," he said, "it being market day and all."

Owen nodded. "*Farmer's Almanac* predicts higher than normal temperatures. Humidity's up. Best get along before we bake to death."

The girls promenaded the sidewalks, accepting samples and pulling pennies from their coin purses. As when they were children, they shared cotton candy and saltwater taffy that clung to their fingers.

"You're sticky enough to draw a hive of bees." I pointed to McFarland's General Store, Papa's commercial endeavor that supplemented his farm income. "Wash up at the faucet behind the store."

When the girls were presentable again, they took in one more round of the booths while Owen and I settled into chairs in front of the store.

Soon Papa joined us. "It's good to have time to talk without the girls around." He turned to Owen. "We're sure thankful Andrew's getting a little better each day."

Owen nodded and smiled. "Your daughter's taking good care of him."

"She learned from the best," Papa replied.

Soon the heat was insufferable, so we piled into the car and aimed for home.

"Whew. I could use a dip in the creek." I wiped my neck and throat. "Wanna go for a swim, girls?"

Their animation brought smiles to our faces.

How their sister would've loved a swim today. Our boys would've enjoyed the same.

Would my little lost ones always linger near?

Back home, I entered our bedroom where Josephine kept vigil over her son.

Bringing his knees to his chest, Andrew held his abdomen and moaned.

I rushed to his side. "What's wrong, dear?"

"He's hungry, of course," she replied.

I kissed Andrew on the forehead. "Won't be long until you can enjoy real food. We're going for a swim before supper." I turned to his mother. "There's broth in the icebox. See you in about an hour." I waved from the doorway and changed for our outing.

After our swim, I joined the girls for a nap while Owen dozed on the divan. A breeze kept a draft moving across the house and fluttered the window sheers like they were wisps of clouds.

Later on, I checked on Andrew. His mother sat beside him in her finery. As far as I knew, she hadn't set down her silk hand-fan all afternoon. I hadn't caught a glimpse of her knitting.

Andrew lay quiet and still. No doubt his mother hadn't let him get in a word, so I didn't worry. I thought I heard him moan a time or two late in the afternoon. Hopefully, I could feed him something worth the effort soon.

At sundown, Owen said, "We'll be on our way now. We're leaving on the train tomorrow morning."

I sighed in relief. "Would you mind dropping off the girls at Mama's? They'll take them to church tonight."

"Of course not," he replied.

I thanked Owen for the day of recreation, and Josephine folded her hand-fan and flounced out.

At bedtime, I turned out the lights and kissed the girls goodnight. As I passed Amaryllis's closed door, a wave of nausea passed through me, and I leaned against the wall. Would the reminders never cease?

Andrew lay in our bed, and I on the cot. Night sounds rose beyond the window screens. Crickets and frogs competed for the moon's attention. His voice, weak and drawn tight, cut through the darkness. "Things unsaid . . . undone."

"Go ahead and say what needs saying. Sounds to me like the crickets have a leg up on the other night singers. Likely as not, you'll bring harmony to the racket."

"Job 13, verse 15."

"Though He slay me, yet will I trust Him?"

"Yes."

"Your thinking cap's working overtime with nothing to keep your hands busy."

He responded with a labored breath. . "Heal breaches."

"Do what?" I asked.

"Psalm 60, second verse. Forgive Frank."

"All right." I figured a simple answer was best at bedtime.

"Under His wings . . . shelter. Psalm 91."

"I understand."

"Our girls . . . Song of . . ."

"Indeed."

"Remember . . . the ebony."

"All right. You keep pointing, and I'll keep looking."

"My soul . . . His."

"Andrew, you're sounding pure morbid. For heaven's sakes, go to sleep."

"Journal . . ."

"The journal in your study?"

I waited, then raised myself to look over the foot of the bed. "Andrew, dear?" He lay on his side, with his hand under his cheek, breathing softly.

Only the night critters answered.

Poor dear. With nothing but broth, he was devoid of strength. I'd talk to Doc about giving him potato gruel tomorrow. "Sleep well, my love."

Sleep wasn't long in coming.

I woke to kitchen sounds. Viola, no doubt. Then it dawned on me. *The sun's shining.* I sat up straight. How in the world could I have slept past sunup?

Flinging the sheet aside, I slipped my feet into slippers and my arms into my wrapper. "Andrew, you must be starving. Shame on me, sleeping in like a lady of leisure."

I tied the wrapper at my waist and slid my feet into slippers. "I believe you didn't move a muscle all night. Turn over here and let me see your handsome face."

He lay as still as bleached stone.

"Andrew?" I laid my hand on his bone-thin shoulder and gave a gentle shake.

I turned his head toward me.

His half-closed eyes stared toward the floor.

I threw the sheet off. The bed was soaked in blood.

A fire started in my belly as a single yellow flame that flared into a blue-hot furnace. My mouth opened to shriek a gruesome "Nooo!"

Viola notified Doc, the Evanses, and Mama and Papa of

Andrew's passing. When Owen and Josephine returned, Viola answered their knock. "Come on in. Uh—"

Josephine's grunt and the slam of the door against the entry wall told me she had pushed her way into the house. Sitting in the quiet of our bedroom, I braced myself for the onslaught. Her hurried footsteps to the bedroom. Her ghastly expression. Her high-pitched shriek.

Owen joined his wife at their son's bedside, his sobs quiet and muffled against the mattress. Soon, she cursed the room and begged him to take her away, and soon they were gone.

Later, Doc explained. "He bled out. Did you feed him something besides water and broth?"

A certain knitting basket came to mind. Then bits of conversations. *I've a hankering for ham and red eye gravy . . . My son needs food . . . If his wife won't feed him, his mother will.*

I rose from the table and walked into the bedroom.

The sewing basket from the previous day sat on the dresser.

I lifted the lid to . . . a covered dish of ham and red eye gravy.

CHAPTER SIXTEEN

Pour out thine indignation upon them,
And let the fierceness of thine anger overtake them.
Psalm 69:24

F ive headstones in a row and me dressed in black. Again. Might as well dig a hole and bury me too for all the good breathing would do.

The church fed the whole countryside after the funeral. It was a dinner on the
ground that he would've enjoyed. Afterward, the family gathered at our house. Folks visited, sang a few songs, prayed, and shed more tears.

I don't recall saying a word, singing a note, or shedding a tear.

Over coming months, my frozen innards mirrored the snow-and-ice-filled days early in the year. Nothing thawed them. Vague forms floated in and out of my room. Nothing brought clarity. I lay on a new mattress, but my mind wandered in a dark, dank space that knew nothing of the light and love that had filled our home.

My heart shriveled like a rotten peach. *He's gone* played and replayed with unmistakable certainty. Andrew's heart had reached into mine, one heart beating for two. Now both lay silent.

I don't have the strength to live for You anymore.

Cade and Lily and their children visited, but their encouragement disappaeared with them.

Owen couldn't tear Josephine away from her son's graveside, so they stayed on three months.

Come mid-May, Viola coaxed me out of my bed—and my stubbornness. "I fixed breakfast. There's biscuits and Mama's famous nectar. Don't you want to get up and eat a bite?"

I mumbled in response. Depression hovered like an ornery horsefly. Sunlight through the window and the sounds of farm life beyond interested me not a whit.

"I'm worth no more than a cast-off cotton sack." I pulled the words from a festering abscess in my heart.

"Listen to yourself!" Viola's cup of frustration appeared to have overflowed. "You have five perfectly beautiful daughters upstairs, and they need you. You have no right to put them through this."

"What do you mean?"

She flung off my sheet. "It's high time you got out of that bed and thought of someone other than yourself."

Hadn't I spoken those very words to Viola myself?

I turned away. "Not today."

"Oh, no you don't. I'm bringing the girls in here, and you're getting dressed."

"No."

"Absolutely yes! Solitude does nothing good for misery. You either get yourself up, or I'll do it for you. Take your pick." McFarland stubbornness glinted in her eyes.

Lacking the strength to resist, I swung my legs over the side of the bed and sat up.

"That's better. Now, let's take this easy. Just stand first, nothing more than that."

Taking her forearm, I eased upward. "The room's swimming." I grabbed my forehead and swayed.

"It'll pass. Give it a minute. I'll help you take one step forward."

She helped me don a cotton wrapper and supported me down the hallway, one shaky step at a time. "Keep looking forward, sis. A body keeps moving in this world by putting one foot in front of the other."

Where had the flighty sister of the past gained such wisdom?

Soon the warmth of home seeped into my bones and wrapped around my heart. It encircled the space and told me I'd mend. I had no choice. The girls needed me. And a bit of news strained to be told.

Sitting at the seldom-used dining table, I ran my fingers through weeks of dust. Someone shut a squeaky door Andrew had never got around to oiling. Life turns on hinges. Mine had turned on wailing hinges more than once. Now that door was closed for good, but I wouldn't let it do me in.

Windblown from their visit at their son's and grandchildren's graves, the Evanses entered the cottage, and Owen trudged in and crumbled into a chair at the table. He stretched his arms across the dusty surface and laid his head between them. His sobs shook his aging frame—and me.

I covered his hands with my own. A ray of sunlight shone on our hands, and lint danced in the beam.

"We'll never recover," he said.

What do you expect of mere dust, Lord?

The back door opened, and Mama and Papa walked in and joined us at the dining table.

"Andrew never got his farm on the banks of the Washita. He always wanted to farm a bit. Did you know that, Mama?"

"Odd, what thoughts come to mind when grief births them. But a body's gotta mourn as it comes."

"I told Andrew he couldn't get blood out of a turnip, any

more than Cade could on his parcel of land." About all my brother accomplished in the fields nowadays was stirring up a passel of dirt devils.

With Viola seeing to them, the girls settled into school at home. The college had supplied assignments, and I had already prepared lesson plans for Ebony and Julia Jane. Their spirits brightened mine. Julia Jane's short curls of the previous year had grown into a mass of long, dark-chocolate ringlets that bounced when she moved. Ebony's rosy mouth spread into deep thumbprints on her cheeks, daring me to remain sober.

Nutrition and the nearness of my girls strengthened me. Gradually, suppertime conversation leapt from one subject to another as if the previous four months hadn't rolled over our heads.

On a bright day in early June, Camellia and Blossom escorted me around the house once and delivered me back to my bedroom. "Thank you for the stroll, girls. It did me good. I'll rest awhile, and then I have some news."

Encircled by my girls, I had shed all thoughts of giving up and dying. From this day forward, I'd look for Andrew's morning stars and listen for their song. I'd mark his words alone in the swing and remember our ordinary things. I'd mark them in our bed, alone, beneath the moon's tender fingers that reached through the window, soothing me, quieting me into sleep.

All of us—the girls and I, Viola and Joshua, Mama and Papa, Cade and his family, and the Evanses—gathered in the family room after supper.

"I've a bit of news."

They quieted and turned their eyes to me.

"I've made nests for nine over the years, and dismantling four has torn my heart to shreds." A flush of warmth started at my breastbone and flashed across my face. "I began to suspect last month, but now I know . . . I may be thirty-eight years old, but it's nest-building time again. Come October, I'm having another baby."

Joy descended in a flood of exclamations, tears, hugs, and slaps on backs. Even Josephine chortled. By the time everyone went their separate ways and the girls had gone to bed, I was ready to tuck myself under the sheets too.

Owen donned his hat and opened the front door to escort his wife away.

"I'd like a word with our daughter-in-law, dear," she said. "Wait for me in the car?"

"All right. See you in the morning, Ella. Our train leaves at noon." He eased the door closed, and his boot heels plunked a subdued farewell and faded into the night.

Josephine turned to me. "I have a request."

"Oh?"

"I'd like to take Julia Jane to Denver tomorrow. She's Andrew's only blood offspring."

I eyed the woman who would have another of my daughters as well as my husband, and I lost all restraint. "Why should I put another of my daughters into your hands?" The charge wasn't fair—Amaryllis hadn't picked up typhoid in Denver— but I shouted it all the same. I itched to hurt her.

Her eyes spread wide, and her skin turned scarlet.

A smoke-belching rail train, I let loose of words I'd suppressed for seventeen years.. "You're a foolish woman. Truth be told, you killed Andrew. You killed your son with ham and red eye gravy, and I'll never forgive you."

She took a step backward.

I clicked open the door, and a warm breeze wrestled with my dress hem. "God forgive me, but I've seen your selfishness and little else over all the years I've known you." I'd lowered my voice to a growl. "Not all of us view life through the lens of a bank account, so you can take your fancy ways, fancy friends, and fancy life and live it far away from me and my girls. I'd as soon be strung up as a horse thief as to lay eyes on you again."

Turning from her, I entered my lonely bedroom. Sat in the rocker. And waited. Before long, the door creaked shut. Owen started his car. And the steady *putt-putt* faded to nothing down the road.

I was rid of Josephine Evans at last.

Sleep didn't come easily. A furnace takes time to cool down. My every ounce of flesh longed to wake and find the other half of me, as strong and tender and wise as before.

I stared a long time at the bead board ceiling.

CHAPTER SEVENTEEN

And they that know thy name will put their trust in thee;
For thou, Jehovah, hast not forsaken them that seek thee.
Psalm 9:10

The blazing heat of summer gave way to the mellow days of autumn.

My three college girls had completed their requirements for the previous term. Considering my coming delivery, they and Ebony returned to Denton on their own for their fourth, third, second, and first years. Andrew and I had agreed our girls would complete four years at CIA, not the usual three. If we'd allowed Amaryllis to graduate her third year, she would've experienced all the joy that attends such an event.

More than one regret pooled in my stomach, as bitter as pond water in a drought.

Nights were the worst.

With chores done and Julia Jane in bed, lights out and time on my hands, and my belly protruding, I often wandered through the house. Memories clanged in my ears. At times, I thought I'd lose my mind. Worst of all, I discovered dark, hard places in my heart that refused to bend. Beasts of selfishness and pride still hollered.

But the eternal Potter reached down to mold me. Again.

First, Cade announced he would take his family south to the Lower Rio Grande Valley of Texas, supposedly a farmer's land of milk and honey. Our region of Oklahoma's persistently lower water table had choked him dry, scattering dust through his dreams. Hail had decimated his tender cotton plants. And an early freeze turned his fall vegetables to mush.

Now I was to relinquish my twin brother, dear sister-in-law, and their children.

Another loss lurks around the corner?

I had no idea at the time that measureless joy awaited me.

With the copse turning shades of russet, chestnut, and gold, heralding the never-ending cycle of life to death and life to come, I swaddled a wriggling piece of Andrew in my arms. It was the twelfth day of October, and Mama had helped Doc attend me.

"We named our first three boys Andrew, Owen, and Gavin, so those names are taken. Your papa was named Micah, Mama."

"No better name. Faithful to the Lord. And never backed down."

I examined my son's dark-brown curls so like Andrew's and his sparkling, blue-marble eyes. "My husband left me a piece of himself in this boy. I want him to grow into the same kind of man. The prophet Micah describes the ideal man in the sixth chapter. 'What doth Jehovah require of thee, but to do justly, and to love kindness, and to walk humbly with thy God?' That describes Andrew. So, Micah it is."

Julia Jane was turning sixteen. No longer a child, she took on the household demands, leaving me the delight of holding my infant against my breast and rocking him for the sheer joy alone.

Days turned into weeks as October drifted into November. The ground outside darkened under the ever-deepening shades of fall, and my girls returned for Thanksgiving. Four of the girls had learned at CIA the technicalities of caring for a newborn and the fifth, and they assured me they were entirely capable. They'd tend to meals and care for their little brother too. I only need nurse and rock him.

Viola swept through the back door the day before Thanksgiving. "All the family's gathering at Mama's and Papa's tomorrow. Time to shuck off pain and count our blessings."

"I have yet to find warmth and love with nothing but memories under my bedcovers." I tapped the end of my son's nose. "But this boy makes up for it."

"Oh . . ."

"Don't worry." I fluttered my fingers. "Weeping is seldom a part of my day now."

"Can you and the girls bring a pot of green beans? Mama and I figure with your cellar packed—"

"For heaven's sakes, Vi, I can open a jar of beans and throw in a ham hock." I paused, mulling. "Is Frank going?"

"Joshua and I would like that. If you're okay with it, that is."

I twisted the idea every which way. My banishment of their Grand Mama had left my girls bereft, and my conscience troubled me. Did I want Frank Irving to blight the rest of my life? Could I trust him around my girls? Not yet. But I could watch him as Andrew would have.

"I won't let the past fracture our family's future. So, yes. I'm okay with it, Vi."

Thanksgiving, the final day of November, dawned clear and cold. The girls and I, with Micah bundled against my chest, flounced through the copse to the McFarland farm.

"Where's Papa?" I handed Micah to Mama, and Blossom set our offering on the table.

Papa tossed his newspaper aside and rose from his reading chair. "Same place as always."

"Happy Thanksgiving, Papa." I kissed his cheek.

"Same to you, daughter. Now that we're all here . . . " He scanned the surroundings and took his place at the large oak table that bore the marks of generations of McFarlands. "I have something to say before we pray."

Our group shushed.

"The Lord's calling Cade and Lily to Texas, and they're leaving us when the weather's cool in December of next year."

I ached at the reminder. The grim prospect of living the rest of my years without the grace-filled presence of my twin and his dear family was almost more than I could stomach.

"What none of you but Cade knows is . . ." He speared us with a piercing gaze. "With farm prices down and the store doing poorly, your mama and I've decided to pull up stakes and go with them."

I frowned in disbelief. "You can't leave. We need you, and you need us."

He nodded in agreement. "True enough. But I hear the Rio Grande Valley's blanketed with hope for the future."

My brother came to his feet. "We're all struggling nowadays. Can't count on farm prices. And with droughts and freezes, trying to make a living farming is like spitting in the wind."

We all chuckled.

"So, I propose all of you consider it." Cade tucked his hands into his pockets.

Stunned, we sat in silence.

Mama grumbled. "This is a shock, but I know in my spirit God's hand is moving in this family. I'm asking you to get on your knees and seek His face. Could be He'd have all of us aim south."

Papa picked up Mama's pitch. "Don't have to decide today. We're looking at a mighty hard decision that, but we all need to make our intentions known soon. As long as we've lived on this place, it'll take the better part of a year to pry our-selves loose."

Viola responded first. "Sounds like an adventure." She turned to her husband. "What do you think, hon?"

Frank looked to his lap and mumbled incoherent syllables. His father had invested his holdings in ill-advised stock just before the start of the Great War and had never recovered his losses. Although the Irvings had supported their daughter-in-law and grandson for many years before they died, Viola's and Frank's prospects looked grim.

Cade took up the clarion call. "The value of my sweat in those acres out back is worth a third of what it was once. Cotton brought thirty-five cents a pound during the war, but I had to settle for twelve cents this year. The church coffers have suffered too, requiring me to both preach in Andrew's place and lead the singing."

All gazes rested on me. Could I abandon the home I'd shared with Andrew? Leave behind my four children buried on the rise? Give up Rock Creek and its songs? And never again lay eyes on Broadview?

"I could never leave this place, but I'll pray about it. For you." I took my place at the table, and my girls followed suit.

Papa eyed me over his spectacles. He opened his mouth as if to speak, but a brisk snap of his napkin told us it was high time we ate. Our patriarch's blessing over the food ended with the first of countless pleas for godly wisdom.

Ma started bowls of greens and potatoes around the table. Platters of turkey and dressing.

Gravy, cranberries, and hot rolls. We spooned and speared in silence, stunned at the surprise Papa had served up.

The McFarland clan would be chewing on this for months.

I excused myself and headed for the creek. More than once over the years, Papa had caught me pondering at the stream. This time he found me fiddling with my apron pocket while mulling over the prospects of living on this land without the rest of the family. I flashed him a halt with an upraised hand. "Don't try to convince me. I'm not going."

"Don't want to add my voice to the commotion spinning in your head. But I'd like to sit and listen to the creek's song. Join me?"

"That'd be fine." My stubborn will straightened my spine.

"Andrew and your four buried children and the home you love, those feelings cut so deep they can get in the way, plug up words, and make it so we can't talk to one another."

I agreed, and like a divine conductor, he coaxed words out of me. He listened with his heart while my words gushed like Turner Falls after a strong spring rain. His heart saw into mine, clear through my pretending.

"All your sorrow is rocks in the creek bed of your life, daughter. Might be time to look elsewhere for another creek, a new song."

The thought left me more than depleted. It left me defeated.

But then joy reached out and starched my britches.

CHAPTER EIGHTEEN

O Jehovah my God, in thee do I take refuge.
Psalm 7:1

1923

Blossom graduated in May. In September, Camellia began her fourth year at CIA; Dahlia, her third; Ebony, her second; and Julia Jane, her first. And I found myself alone, doting on my toddler.

Thankfully, Blossom had returned home and landed a job with *Needham News*.

Finally, I could venture into Andrew's study.

I woke to a barn swallow's song the first morning of October. I'd found the writing material Andrew had poured over in his study, his journal, but had yet to make it through to the end. Stepping onto the porch with the dogeared diary, I settled into the swing.

He had carved notes on every page. His pen scratching flamed in margins. It flowed in neat, spare letters on some pages and cut a fierce scrawl on others. I heard his voice and felt his passion in every word.

Then I read his final entry.

> 6 February 1922
> Ella Jane,
> If the Lord takes me before you, don't give up.

Make a new life for yourself and the girls. Too many memories around here. Stay in the shadow of His wings. That's where you'll find shelter—and me.

I'll love you through eternity,
Andrew

P.S. Remember the ebony and Psalm 91. And forgive Frank and Mother. Heal the breaches. Do it for me.

I folded in upon myself and let out a howl.

Later, standing before the mantel with my arms hanging at my sides, as limp as days-old lettuce, I stared at the ebony.

A longing for Andrew's presence, his affection and wisdom, took me to my knees. Suddenly, a groundswell of need for the Lord outstripped every other desire. For the first time in my life, I fell to my face on the braided rug and cried out, "I have no refuge but you. Show me your face."

Micah, my handsome, raven-haired boy, bawled from his room, and I dried my eyes.

Thereafter, when I took to the swing and set it to swaying each morning, I sat with Psalm 91 in my lap. Some days I read it aloud through clenched teeth and others, while I wept. But I read it. And in almost imperceptible stages, the Lord changed my heart.

On the twenty-ninth day of November, seventeen McFarlands, counting my six children, stood around my table. Before us lay fare that duplicated Thanksgiving the previous year.

I cleared my throat, and the chatter quieted. "Before we begin, I have an announcement. The girls and I talked this over." I nodded toward my beautiful five. "We've all decided.

Our four college girls will return to CIA, but Blossom, Micah, and I will go with you to the Valley."

The group took a collective breath and heaved it out.

"I vowed years ago that Andrew's investments would rear our girls and do good for others. Our daughters are all but grown, and three institutions—the home for unwed mothers, the one for war widows, and Jackson Academy for orphans—will continue to benefit from the trusts we set up for them. Now I'm down to what Andrew left me, and I've Micah to rear and educate. I have enough to buy a plot of land. Maybe I can fulfill Andrew's dream of farming.

"So, I cast our lots with you and trust God to provide. Blossom, Micah, and I will travel with you, and when the other girls graduate, they'll follow. If they choose to, of course." A tear sneaked out one eye. "I don't want to live here without you."

Papa's head dropped forward. Then he glanced around our circle. "Let's all bow our heads and thank God for His bounty."

The family said amen in unison and laid out declarations of gratitude as surely as the homegrown trimmings around our platter of ham. Papa gathered up the praise offerings and made a declaration of his own.

"It's a long way to the southernmost tip of Texas. Can't afford to ship our possessions by rail. Even tickets for thirteen of us would cut into our funds. So—with Frank's help—we located four covered wagons and horses to pull them."

Viola gasped. "Covered wagons? In 1923?"

"We'll likely present a spectacle. But we haven't a choice. We've marked off the route to the west of us. It's part graded, part graveled, and part under construction. The weather'll warm up the farther south we go. And in two months' time, baring bad weather, we should pull into Red Fish Landing, south of the famed King Ranch. We'll feed ourselves on the sea's bounty while we find land to settle."

Good. We'll settle near our dear friends, Adelaide and Brady Duvall.

I decided to take bare essentials and close up the cottage intact. The girls could return as they saw fit to remove their possessions. With Rowena Maddox Home for Women and Children just the other side of the creek and my friend Adelaide's home for war widows just a stone's throw away in one wing of nearby Broadview, I wouldn't worry.

That evening a knock at the front door called me from Micah's room. I had just kissed him goodnight.

I peeked outside. Was that Viola's Studebaker? I flung open the door. "Welcome, sis—"

Frank, slouching with his hands in his pockets, straightened and hooked a thumb over his belt. "Hope I've not come too late."

Movement drew my gaze to the idling automobile where my sister sat staring.

Soon I'd be setting out across country in the company of this man. Might as well start tamping down my disgust. "Why don't you and Vi come inside?"

He glanced back at his wife. "Can we sit out here on the porch?"

Good idea. His wife can keep an eye on him.

I took the swing, and he grabbed a wicker chair. Even in late November, a night bug flittered around the porch light.

"What is it, Frank?"

"I've come to apologize."

"To please your wife?"

"Not only Vi. For me, too."

"And what exactly do you have to apologize for?"

An unfamiliar expression flashed across the rascal's features. Was it humility? "First, what I did to you years ago."

"You mean when you tried to steal my innocence?"

His chin dropped toward his chest. "That was the first thing."

"What else?" I refused to let him off the hook without articulating exactly what he'd done to me and my family.

"Running off with your sister."

"To spite me."

He shrugged. "That was it at the time, but eighteen years later, I know what a peach I married."

"She's been loyal, even while the state of Oklahoma kept you behind bars."

"You're right. Her and Joshua's visits meant the world. Those were cruel years."

I tipped my head forward and eyed him under a peaked eyebrow. "For more of us than just you."

"I know that. And I'm sorry you've had to endure so much. You've proven your mettle."

Inhaling a goodly portion of night air, I allowed my shoulders to collapse. "Is that all?"

He peered at me with ink-black eyes. "You know it isn't."

"What is it then? Get it off your chest, Frank. Go on. Tackle it like a man."

"All right. I'm sorry about what I did to Andrew."

"You've paid your debt, thanks to the Oklahoma State Penitentiary."

"Yeah, but that doesn't wipe the slate clean. I owe you a debt."

"You don't owe me a speck of anything, Frank. Except to take care of my sister and nephew."

"That's what I intend to do. But I gotta try to clear the air. Square things up—"

"You'll never make things right, if that's what you're thinking. Some things are beyond fixing."

"I understand. But I have to say this anyway. If I could go back and redo what I did as a jealous young man . . . if I could hear just one more of Andrew's sermons . . . if I could trip and fall into those saw blades in his place . . . I would. I'll regret that evil the rest of my days."

He strode off the porch toward the car.

Viola opened her door, hopped over the running board, and loped up the stairs. "We've reconciled, sister. But I have yet to speak some words I've thought for a couple of decades."

Sitting there on my front porch, staring at the man who'd bedeviled my life, I asked the Lord to forgive him. And—quite unexpectedly—a weight lifted from around my heart.

Andrew would nod and assure me, "I'm proud of you, dear."

A bundle of hard feelings—and not just for Frank—rolled away that night. High time.

CHAPTER NINETEEN

Blessed is he whose transgression is forgiven,
Whose sin is covered.
Psalm 32:1

Viola stood in my kitchen with a saucepan in her hands and two crates of kitchenware at her feet.

"Impossible to live here without you and every soul I love." I chuckled. "Had to be stubborn before I gave in."

She threw me one of her *you beat all* looks, packed the saucepan, and picked up the iron. "I'm as tickled as a bee in clover. Proud you're letting go of the past and trusting God with the future."

"It remains to be seen how well I trust. Since I took to getting on my face before the Lord, He's been parceling out peace."

"I suspect Andrew's up yonder reminding Him every single day."

"Wouldn't surprise me."

She raised her brows in a question. "Want to go to the cemetery one last time?"

"No, I've said my goodbyes and shed all the tears I intend to on those five mounds." I returned to packing. "But grief can settle over me like a dust cloud at times. Sure you want to share the road with Oklahoma dust?"

"I won't travel a road you aren't on, sis. So, hush up

about dust, and let's get to packing." She sashayed to the fire-place and removed the ebony from the mantel. "You aren't going to Texas without this. It's the whole family's Ebenezer now."

"I'm waiting until the last minute to pack it."

She offered me a warm, generous smile. The lamplight shone brilliant golden against her dark chestnut eyelashes.

"You're dazzling, Vi."

"I'm nothing of the sort."

Granted, Viola had once flaunted her beauty, but sixteen years of being labeled a prisoner's wife and visiting her husband behind bars had taken a toll. "That's part of what makes you dazzling. You don't know you are."

She *humphed*. "Not anymore."

"You leave me speechless at times."

She leaned toward me, and golden-brown strands tumbled over her shoulders. "You, speechless? Now I know you're joshing."

We chuckled with the familiarity years of love breed. Sitting on the floor, we leaned against the wall.

I took her hand. "How you've grown, sis."

"Aw, I have you to thank."

I flinched sideways. "Me? Why, I was a thorn in your flesh for years."

"I tried not to show it, but I watched and listened. Just too stubborn to admit it. But after tagging along after you and finding myself the wife of a prisoner, I realized I was in need of a thorough cleansing myself. That's what Jesus offers—a bath, a new set of clothes, and a place of honor beside Him. I accepted Christ because I first saw Him in you."

"I'm thankful, Vi," I said, holding back tears. "Truly."

"I was born with a name folks respect. But then I ran off and married the scoundrel of the county, which earned me everyone's disrespect. Now you've accepted me and even Frank back into the fold."

I put my arm around her shoulders and squeezed.

"I'm finally at peace, Ella. And I'm praying for your contentment and that you'll forgive even Josephine. It'll do you a world of good."

I shivered. "Don't expect too much. I'm just dust. Remember."

She quirked her head to the side. "Yeah, but you're *His* dust."

Standing, I opened my arms. "I love you, dear one."

"I love you, too, sis."

In her rare amber eyes, I found a world of hope. I knew without foresight that she and I would remain near to one another the rest of our days.

She cleared her throat and forced back her shoulders. "We have weeks of travel facing us, ample time to get into the whys and why-nots of what drove a wedge between us. But I wanted to open the door to talking before we set out."

"Alright, Vi."

"Frank was a rank criminal, but years in prison and his folks dying in that awful train wreck left him a broken man. I'm sure he told you he can't forgive himself for all the hurt he caused. Now I'm wondering if you'll forgive me too. I was dreadfully prideful, selfish, and jealous. Can we learn to be sisters in the truest sense?"

I grabbed her in a firm embrace. "With the Lord's help. Looks to me like He's got His angels working overtime already. We're likely to face thunderstorms on the road to Texas, but as Andrew always said, we'll shelter under His wings."

At the back door after a long day of packing, Viola raised her eyes to the heavens. "Just look at you, big ol' Oklahoma sky. You've traded your silver day dress for an evening gown of violet-gray."

"Hmm. And the last sunrise'll come tomorrow. . Andrew isn't here to handle the team, grease the axle, or shod a horse, but I figure his 'stubbornest female on God's green earth' suffragist wife can do it herself."

She chuckled and stepped through the brown grass toward the trail.

"Thanks for helping, Vi."

She waved back and faded into the shadows toward their home across the way.

How many times had I stood in this spot and waved to a loved one? No telling. But if I was to *ride* with them—not wave at them—I'd better get to bed.

My purposeful stride took me across the wooden floorboards and into the dining room.

A solitary hatbox sat on the table. Painted roses and ribbons, hand fans and pearls adorned its surface. I cradled it in my arms and knelt beside the cedar chest glowing in the lamplight. I removed items that would serve as my Ebenezers in Texas. Our wedding portrait. An anniversary platter. A mirror from a distant Christmas. And a shaving set I'd given Andrew.

Uncovering his worn journal, I opened it, and the pages fluttered like a startled covey of quail. "I'll continue our story, dear. Taking plenty of lamp oil for reading and writing."

I wrapped the Ebenezers in cotton batting and returned them to the box. Opening the chest, I laid my vault of memories between handmade quilts. My own now-blank journal would ride on top.

Closing the chest, I ran my fingers across the inlaid prairie flowers and precious words—*Ella's Treasures*—Papa had carved into the wood. "Travel well, sweet memories."

An automobile's purr interrupted my musings, and I peeked through the curtains.

Who could that be?

A man and woman, their heads lowered. Untidy silver hair. Pale skin. The woman's fingers worrying a hat. A box under the man's arm, his other arm draped around her waist.

As I opened the door, they lifted their heads.

What were Josephine and Owen doing at my front door?

I flung open the door. "What're you two doing here?"

Owen nudged Josephine, and she forced her gaze from the floor. "Can't let you leave for the wilderness without loving on Blossom and Micah." I'd sent them Micah's birth announcement and a portrait the previous Mother's Day. "Nor without settling accounts with you."

I opened the door wide and prepared for a dressing-down. "Come on in."

We settled on the divan and matching armchairs, and she dived into what was eating her. "I'm sorry for the hard feelings I've caused."

A I had to force my mouth not to drop open and gathered myself. "I can be sharp-tongued, bossy, and willful as a mule."

"You've been perfectly genteel, dear. You loved and cared for Andrew." She dabbed a hankie at her nostrils. "I'm the one who's been sharp-tongued and bossy. Will you forgive me?"

Not the prideful matron of yesteryear but a frail, broken woman pled for my forgiveness.

I nodded. "If you'll forgive me."

She waved away my suggestion. "We've visited the girls in Denton."

My eyes widened, and my chin dropped. All this time the girls had been at CIA, their grandparents had visited them not a single time.

"We've missed them. And wanted to see them in their college environment. My, what wonderful girls you and Andrew reared."

I nodded, astounded at what I was seeing and hearing.

She continued. "I'm leaving my grandmother's china tea set to Julia Jane, but I'm handing it to you for safekeeping."

"Delicate china might not be safe in a wagon."

"We're getting way up in years," Owen said. "Likely won't be around much longer." He handed over the satin-wrapped box. "Tell her how much love this represents."

I accepted the gift, and tears crowded the back of my eyes.

"We wrote notes, told her love's beautiful like china. When she's some lucky man's wife, I want her to enjoy this set," Josephine said. "But like love, it's delicate. She must handle it with care."

I brushed away a memory I'd long bottled up. Mama had given Julia Jane what she called a china tea set. In reality, it was made of inexpensive crockery.

Josephine had been present that day and had spoken to Julia Jane in hushed tones. "Is it a *china* set, dear?"

"China?" the eight-year-old had asked.

How's a mere girl to know the difference?

"Fine dishes are made of china. Ordinary dishes are . . . well, they're ordinary." She turned over the little teapot. "This was made in Mexico. I'll give you *real* china one day."

China, my foot.

Mama had advised me to pray for Josephine, but all these years later, I couldn't remember speaking a single word on my mother-in-law's behalf.

They visited with Blossom and Micah upstairs, and when they drove away, they took a part of me with them.

CHAPTER TWENTY

Weeping may tarry for the night,
But joy cometh in the morning.
Psalm 30:5

I wandered around the house with a mug of coffee and a candle lamp, recalling the bounteous love that had flourished within these walls. And in the hearts of those who had gone before. My grandparents who had planted roots deep in the Father's love. Andrew's aunt and uncle who had first welcomed me into their family. The dear preacher and his wife who had fed our souls. Broadview's protective overseer and its house-keeper. And Frank's parents, who had embraced Viola and Joshua so well.

Andrew showed up everywhere.

I stepped onto the front porch and brushed my fingers over the bittersweet vine that trailed the trellis and posts. "You're a fine old house, my friend. Solid and sturdy. You've weathered many a storm. Thank you, home of my heart. I'll miss you."

I'd once wondered if we could make the Hanson girls our own . . . if we could give our six beloved daughters the life they deserved . . . if I could send them into the world with all its dangers and allurements . . . and if I could go on if anything happened to even one of them.

With Andrew's love and support, we'd accomplished the first two, and I'd made a good start on the last two.

When I opened Andrew's study, his hand guided mine. I walked inside, and his arm rested on my shoulder. I aimed for his desk, and his heels *kerplunk*ed with mine. And when I pulled out his office chair, he scooted one alongside me.

My journal lay on the desk.

When I turned up the lamp wick, his finger pointed to where I would document the coming years. How would it compare to his record?

The precise script in his journal dated from our wedding day in 1905 to the seventh day of February 1922.

My name showed up on every page.

Make me worthy of Ella McFarland.

Show Ella how You work all things for our good and Your glory.

Give Ella trust in Your goodness.

I hadn't realized how fully Andrew had loved me. His understanding of God was part and parcel of his love for me. The more he had loved Jesus, the more he had loved me. The better he had understood the Almighty, the better he had understood me. The firmer his grasp of God's grace, the fuller his graciousness had grown toward me.

Andrew's purity, faith, and wisdom had set me back on my heels more than once in our life together. He understood and lived all three. God had left His handprint all over my Andrew.

I dipped my pen into the inkwell and touched the tip to the page.

17 December 1923

Dearest Andrew,
Soon the dawn will be upon us. The children

and I are leaving Oklahoma. We'll travel with all the family in a train of covered wagons. Imagine that. Every inch of me aches for you. But when we pull out, I'm as determined as an ornery mule to sing along with the morning stars.

I'll love and miss you always,
Ella

P.S. You can relax. I mended the breaches, and I'm taking the ebony. Leaving whole. Will try to do a little farming down south near the Rio Grande. For you.

Next morning, a covered wagon rattled up with Cade on the driver's seat. He positioned it in front of mine where Blossom, Micah, and Shaker awaited me. Two other wagons, with Papa and Frank at the reins, parked third and fourth in line.

Papa jumped down, and all the wagons' occupants followed. They formed a semicircle in front of my porch.

The five steps to the ground punctuated the end of one journey and the beginning of the next. Blossom brought me Micah, and I faced the family who loved me so well.

"There's no way I can express my gratitude for the love you've shared over the years right here on this soil, what you've meant to me and to Blossom and her sisters in Denton, all of them little women now, and to Micah, although he doesn't appreciate it yet."

Chuckles rounded the semicircle.

I pointed toward the graveyard. "And to my five beloved ones on the rise. Andrew thanks you for cradling us on this journey to Texas. If he were here . . ." I turned my eyes to the heavens. "He'd insist I walk arm-in-arm with my eternal husband. I'll do my best."

Papa stepped forward and stood alongside me. Gazing at the morning star-studded heavens, he placed one hand on Micah's dark crown, raised the other toward the skies, and spoke the family blessing in his deep, resonant voice.

"We offer up to You, Lord, Micah McCowan Evans, the fruit of generations of faith. May he tell of Your goodness to the generations who follow from this day forward and forever. Amen, amen, and amen."

We shouted and took to our separate, canvas-topped homes-away-from-home.

"Giddy up!" My brother clicked his tongue and snapped the reins.

I flicked the strips of leather in my hands, and the horses plodded toward the dawn. Tossing a kiss to the little graveyard, I urged the team forward.

In my imagination, I curled up on the swing with Andrew, and we talked of ordinary things. The soft kisses of damselflies on still water. The warmth of the May sun bringing forth new life. And Jesus putting my shattered heart and limping faith back together again.

ABOUT THE AUTHOR

Linda Brooks Davis is a lifelong Texan. Her children and six grandchildren were born in Texas, and she devoted the bulk of her 40 years as a special educator to Texas schools. Her mother and grandmother hailed from Oklahoma, the setting for Linda's 2015 debut novel, *The Calling of Ella McFarland*--Book One in the Women of Rock Creek series--which won the 2014 Jerry Jenkins Operation First Novel Award and the 2016 American Christian Fiction Writers Carol Award as. *Soon the Dawn* provides a bridge between the first series and the second, Valley of Promise. Linda writes from her home in San Antonio, Texas, where she and her beloved husband Al worship and minister at Oak Hills Church. Readers may contact Linda through her website lindabrooksdavis.com.

HISTORICAL NOTES

In *Soon the Dawn*, I continue my mother's and grandmother's storytelling tradition through imaginary people and places, the circumstances of certain characters' lives, historical realities, and my ancestors' overcoming of tragedy and loss through faith and grit.

Needham, Westwood, Fair Valley, Glover County, Rock Creek and its rural environs, Broadview, and Christ Church are imaginary, as are the characters themselves. The Lower Rio Grande Valley and Red Fish Landing are true geographical locations, although Red Fish Landing is now known as Port Mansfield. (https://tshaonline.org/handbook/online/articles/hrpaq)

College of Industrial Arts in Denton, Texas—my deceased mother- in-law Charlotte Camille Lane Davis's alma mater—truly existed and lives on today. Established in 1901 by an act of the Texas Legislature, it became known as Girls' Industrial College in 1903 and conferred its first degrees in 1904. The college changed its name to College of Industrial Arts in 1905 and today is known as Texas Woman's University.

I grew up knowing my mother's cedar chest was off limits. It contained priceless treasures: Mother's and Daddy's wedding suits. An old, tattered quilt. Mother's felt hat with a jaunty feather at the rolled-up brim. Bible notes. An old platter and a man's shaving set. A stained tablecloth. Equally stained ladies' handkerchiefs. And old crocheted and scorched potholders. These are the inspiration for the items Ella examines in her cedar chest.

The account of Amaryllis's and Andrew's deaths is based on my grandmother's lifelong stories about her own experience in losing her husband, William Tribble Banks, and daughter, Eula Banks, to typhoid fever in 1922. Andrew's manner of death reflects the reality of my Papa's passing. I pray I've presented the tragic events my grandmother endured in a respectful way that honors her faith and grit.

The McFarland clan's packing up and moving to Texas in covered wagons in 1923 is a retelling of my Pyle family's true experience. Their tale continues in the coming Valley of Promise stories.

I alone am responsible for any factual or historical errors in *Soon the Dawn*. They result not by design but by frailty.

AUTHOR ACKNOWLEDGMENTS

One story sprouts readily while another requires the heart to break, the spirit to bend, and a spring of tears to flow. This is one of those. It originates in the true-life story of my grandmother Mama, Ella Jane Pyle Banks Knox. Waiting in the shadows for close to a century, it is now exposed to the renewing power of the light of Jesus Christ. May He accomplish His purposes on these pages.

Thank you, Sharon Bales of Elmore City, Oklahoma. Fifteen years ago, you welcomed Al and me to the State Bank where I caught an imaginary glimpse of my grand- and great-grandparents making deposits at the same teller's window.

Thank you, Julia Embree of the Pauls Valley Library in Pauls Valley, Oklahoma. You graciously showed me around the historical section and whetted my appetite.

Thank you, J.R. McCaskill, a newly discovered cousin who showed Al and me around the land our ancestors once inhabited. The old cemetery where our common great-great-grandparents, Samuel and Catharine Pyle, are buried returns in my memory as I write these words. Your hospitality and graciousness remain with me.

Thank you, Evelyne Labelle of Carpe Librum Book Design for the beautiful cover. Not only are you proficient, but you're patient beyond measuring.

Thank you, members of my support team (Teresa Brooks, Caryl McAdoo, Carole Clinton, Wendy Kell, Jean Volk, Ann Ferri, Phyllis Rundell, Pam Whorwell, Connie Porter Saunders, Betti Mace, Ann Tatlock, Dawn Kinzer, Clarice G. James, Dave

Parks, Lana Christian, Phyllis Clark Nichols, John M. Cunningham, Jr, Jennifer Smith, Polly Lewis, Emily Adney, and Becky Gifford Smith) for your support of my work.

Thank you, Michaela Mencacci, for sharing your knowledge of social media and moderating the Linda Brooks Davis & Friends Support Group. You are an answered prayer.

Thank you, Sarah Krening, for your keen editor's eye and on-target suggestions that made this story better. You're good for me.

Thank you, Teresa Billingsley Brooks, for epitomizing a sister-in-love. You have prayed without ceasing for me and my work. My gratitude knows no bounds.

Thank you, Mama, for leaving a grandmother's legacy fit for me to pass on. I wish I had known way back then what I know now. I'd visit you more often, hug you tighter, write you more faithfully, and tell you I love you in a hundred ways.

Thank you, Mother—Goldie Leona Banks Brooks. Nowhere in God's creation did a truer, nobler, nor fuller human love exist than yours. You insisted on what I needed, not what was popular. Looked out for me like the ever-hovering blackbirds over the cornfield. And hesitated not a moment to appear unannounced and uninvited at events for which I'd gone past curfew. Your unfeigned faith in Jesus Christ dwelt first in your mother, Ella Jane, and in her mother, Louisa. I pray I'm handing down a faith no less true, honorable, and brave. Your love of family roots and your stories have waited patiently to be told. I hope this story meets your approval. My heart remembers. It always will.

Thank you, Daddy, for the sterling example of Jesus you set every single day. Your patience in suffering, nobility of spirit, and astounding wisdom will remain in my memory as long as I breathe.

Thank you, Al Davis—husband mine—for your love that paints a beautiful dawn every day of life.

Above all, thank You, Lord Jesus. You alone are the Eternal Creator of Dawns.

AUTHOR NOTES

You first met Ella McFarland Evans in award-winning *The Calling of Ella McFarland*, a story set in 1905 Indian Territory prior to Oklahoma statehood.

In *A Christmas to Remember*, Ella and her husband Andrew anticipated Christmas 1908 in their cottage on the banks of Rock Creek. Three years into their marriage, they and their life had changed. What could have prepared them for the challenges thus far? Or those ahead? In this *Gift of the Magi*-inspired story, Ella is transformed. Again.

I hope *Soon the Dawn* blesses you. The import of reader feedback can't be overstated. So I thank you in advance for your review on Amazon and Goodreads and your recommendations on social media.

Inspired by my mother's love beyond reckoning and by knowledge of the grief endured by my grandmother, Ella Jane Pyle Banks Knox, I tithe in her memory a portion of the proceeds from *The Calling of Ella McFarland*, *A Christmas to Remember*, and *Soon the Dawn* to the cause of Christ.

Sign up at lindabrooksdavis.com for my weekly blog with bi-monthly author interviews and giveaways and my quarterly newsletter. I love to hear from readers on my Facebook Author Page, Linda Brooks Davis; Twitter @LBrooksDavis; and on my website.

LINDA

I have not stopped giving thanks for you
Ephesians 1:16

www.ingramcontent.com/pod-product-compliance
Lightning Source LLC
Chambersburg PA
CBHW020251150626
46552CB00020B/771